For an angry instant she hated him

"Reid," Joanna said, mastering her emotion, "I know my design was rejected and someone else got the job."

"You never learn," he said with a sigh. "I've told you and told you to leave the business end of the deal to me. I wonder when I've ever given you occasion to doubt—"

"Reid," she cut him off. "Why beat a dead horse with your lies? You put me up, helped me train and kept me busy all summer—in more ways than one. But all good things must come to an end."

"What's that supposed to mean?"

"The next time you see me, if ever, will be on television."

"You'll have me to thank for that, in part," he said.

"It's thanks to you I was injured in the first place!" Joanna spat back. "Haven't you done enough?"

Books by Donna Huxley

HARLEQUIN PRESENTS
754—INTIMATE
776—NUMBER ONE

These books may be available at your local bookseller.

Don't miss any of our special offers. Write to us at the
following address for information on our newest releases.

Harlequin Reader Service
P.O. Box 52040, Phoenix, AZ 85072-2040
Canadian address: P.O. Box 2800, Postal Station A,
5170 Yonge St., Willowdale, Ont. M2N 6J3

DONNA HUXLEY

number one

Harlequin Books

TORONTO • NEW YORK • LONDON
AMSTERDAM • PARIS • SYDNEY • HAMBURG
STOCKHOLM • ATHENS • TOKYO • MILAN

Harlequin Presents first edition April 1985
ISBN 0-373-10776-5

Original hardcover edition published in 1984
by Mills & Boon Limited

PROLOGUE

MANY months later, when it was all over and behind her, she would be grateful for life itself.

With a shudder she would recall that her very existence had been at stake that bright morning when the struggle began.

How silently our nightmares steal upon us, she would muse. On shafts of gay spring sunshine their first dark threads creep forward, coiling around us with furtive stealth even as we breathe in the cool air of day, a carefree smile on our lips.

Indeed, death itself had been at her elbow that first morning.

But she had not died. Instead she had awakened to a new world of searing pain and numb oblivion, and sudden ecstasies too enchanting to describe or to forget.

Once begun it had seemed endless, that infinity of joys and sorrows rearing before her all at once like a strange, foreign fate. Yet it was hers. How could she say no to it, when its sinuous paths opened within her own breast?

And when she pondered its unseen approach, a single instant hung hard and luminous before her memory. It was the last instant of a placid, ordered life whose time had run out.

There was a face in the mirror. But it was not her own face.

Then everything shattered as the future closed in.

CHAPTER ONE

THE tumult of stunned applause had died abruptly, and a hush of almost unbearable anticipation hung in the air above Pine Trail Golf Club's hallowed eighteenth green. A gallery of over five thousand, joined by millions of television viewers, fixed its eyes on a tiny dimpled ball which lay on the close-cut, rolling slope not twelve feet from the hole.

The television image magnified the little white sphere to huge proportions. Behind it Bermuda grass glowed like jade in the shade of the huge old oaks whose presence offered the sweltering spectators some relief from the unseasonable heat of this last Sunday in May. In the distance, the ranks of North Carolina long-leaf pines lining the fairway shone only as an out-of-focus background, dark and rather foreboding.

The camera's enormous blow-up of the ball was not as absurd as it seemed, for this was the last hole of the final round of the prestigious Southern Invitation tournament—certainly the most important event on the L.P.G.A. tour at this time of year—and the result of this ball's movement towards the hole would determine the outcome of the championship.

'It's all up to Joanna now,' the network commentator announced dramatically from his position high in the TV tower behind the green. 'After seventeen holes in a deadlock for the lead at eight under par, with no other players even close, she appeared to have the tournament in her pocket only two minutes ago. Peggy Byrne had put her ball in the bunker and seemed sure to make bogey. But as you can see in the replay,' he said as the image divided into a split-screen, 'true to her reputation as a clutch player, Peggy made the amazing happen.'

On the left side of the screen Peggy Byrne, the venerable holder of forty-seven tour titles and a great favourite among fans, was shown in slow motion, blasting her half-buried ball out of the bunker in a high arc that landed it on the slope above the hole. Zooming quickly to watch the ball trickle down the incline, closer and closer to the flagstick, the camera caught the magic and improbable moment when hundreds of hands raised skyward in shock and delight among the cardboard periscopes in the gallery to salute its disappearance into the cup.

Through her miracle shot Peggy had turned a sure bogey into a birdie, and thus put all the pressure on her opponent.

The replay image stopped in freeze frame as Peggy's plump, athletic figure was shown climbing out of the bunker. With her patented cheerful grin she waved to the astounded crowd.

On the right side of the screen a pair of tanned legs had moved into position beside the motionless ball on the green. In a patch of sunlight their shapely ankles and slender calves glowed golden brown above white golf shoes. Before them hung the stainless steel shaft of a putter whose offset aluminium head was now poised behind the ball.

'A few moments ago,' the commentator went on as Peggy's frozen smile receded and disappeared, 'it looked as though a par would win the tournament for Joanna. Now she must make this twelve-foot birdie putt to force a play-off, or Peggy will win the championship outright.'

The putter head stirred imperceptibly as the fascinated camera moved slowly upward along the shaft, past the soft curve of willowy female thighs to a pale lavender skirt and a pair of slender hands curled with almost surgical delicacy around the club's rubber grip.

The image slid higher to reveal two brown arms and bare shoulders emerging from a white cotton tank top whose fabric hugged the gentle swell of rounded breasts underneath. The camera's languorous ascent heightened the impression of lithe tensile strength almost coyly concealed behind the sweet, lissome contours of this already famous figure.

A ponytail held flowing blonde hair, bleached already by the sun of the spring tour, away from gold-flecked green eyes that darted calmly from the ball beneath them to the target twelve feet away. They were quiet eyes, reflective and even vulnerable under fine arched brows. Yet in their depths glimmered iron discipline and total concentration.

Thin but sensual lips, pursed slightly in this tense moment, and a creamy complexion burnished by long days spent in the sun, completed the unique and much-admired image of Joanna Lake.

Though a long shot of her stance at address would have identified her instantly to a knowledgeable observer, the networks' directors, always aware of the fans' fascination with her unusual beauty and unmarried status, could never resist caressing her visually whenever she was the focus of drama, as today.

'I'm sure none of us would like to be in Joanna's shoes right now,' the announcer's murmuring voice continued. 'She's played a brilliant tournament, as always, but this time she must have been sure that victory just couldn't slip away. Yet that's what will happen unless the consistency she's famous for gets her through this putt.'

The tension in his voice echoed the torn emotions of the gallery and of the millions of viewers listening to him. Peggy Byrne, the courageous veteran who had survived a life-threatening kidney ailment ten years ago and gone on to win great victories, was on the way to her personal goal of fifty tour titles, and everyone wanted her to reach it before injury or passing time forced her to retire.

But Joanna Lake, famed for the perfection of her swing and her disciplined approach to her profession, was no less a heroine to legions of fans. She had entered the tour seven years ago at the tender age of twenty-one, not long after the break-up of a precocious, unsuccessful marriage whose only legacy was her infant daughter. As time passed her fiercely independent personality and dedication to her child became well-known aspects of her public persona.

No less celebrated was the mystery of her performance on the L.P.G.A. tour. In seven years she had won the Vare Trophy for lowest stroke average three times, and had been leading money winner twice. Yet, incredibly, she had won only three tour events in her entire career, and none in decisive fashion. Though she was considered one of the top women pros in ratings and in earnings, victory always seemed to elude her.

The conundrum that was Joanna Lake's golf game only seemed to underline the appeal of her natural, unpretentious beauty, for it added a tinge of vulnerability to her reputation as perhaps the most dependably competitive player on the entire tour.

Her marriage, ancient history now, had left her a lovely and vibrant young mother, supremely eligible and proudly self-sufficient. Sports publications, their editors regretful that her lack of tour victories prevented them from presenting her on their covers more often, seized whatever occasions they could to publish articles about her as 'the L.P.G.A.'s best-kept secret' or 'golf's quietest sex symbol'.

Thus a groundswell of excitement had erupted only minutes ago when it seemed that Joanna was at last to break through in her first important championship. Perhaps, it was hoped, her always fine efforts would begin to be crowned with victory.

But again she was in danger of losing.

If any of these thoughts were in her mind as she stood over her ball, they were not visible in the calm, motionless features of her face. So deep was her concentration that she was unaware of the millions of eyes fixed admiringly to her slender form, and of the myriad hopes and fears that made her the focus of so much attention.

Nor was she consciously aware that a single pair of eyes, indifferent to the crowd's expectations, was focused upon her with particular intensity.

Slowly the putter head moved back from the ball.

'Whatever the outcome,' the commentator was saying, 'this round will certainly go down as the most thrilling closing round in the history of this championship, and as the most exciting finish we've broadcast this year.'

As he spoke a camera high in the tower showed Joanna bent over the ball. Twelve feet from her the flagstick swayed in the warm breeze. Then the close-up returned. The putter's head was moving forward now, suspended with perfect tempo over the bent grass carpet, striking the ball firmly in its passage.

Now the camera beyond the hole watched the ball roll as unseen hands removed the pin, watched Joanna's eyes follow the roll as thousands of hearts leapt in the huge, silent gallery.

She had struck the putt flawlessly. The ball moved a bit to the right to make up for the break caused by the slope. Then it began to curve back, back into the line leading into the cup's dark depth.

But the hot sun had baked the bent grass more than Joanna or her caddy had anticipated over the course of the afternoon. The green was a trifle faster than it had been all week.

Her ball, moving a shade too fast, lipped the cup, began to fall, was forced upward by its own momentum, and spun off to the right as the stunned crowd, sure it was going to go in, roared its collective split-second convulsion from joy to disappointment.

Waves of impotent sympathy seemed to flow from the gallery towards Joanna's fragile figure. But respectful and even delighted cheers for Peggy Byrne were already beginning to be heard, for her victory was something to celebrate.

Minutes later, having congratulated Peggy and accepted her winnings with a smile as dozens of cameras clicked their attention to her photogenic beauty, Joanne was on her way to the locker room, her mind absorbed by a single thought.

She could hardly wait to call Tina.

A determined group of reporters stopped her before she could reach the clubhouse. Though she knew what their questions would be, and had answered them a thousand times before at dozens of other tournaments, she was cheerful and even humorous in reply.

'Joanna,' a well-known sports writer said, 'you seem to have continued your tradition of brilliant second-place finishes here today. Are you disappointed to have come so close without winning?'

'Not at all,' Joanna shook her head. 'When Peggy makes a shot like the one she played out of that bunker, there's nothing you can do but take your hat off to her and be glad you were there to see it. She has her own way with a sand wedge, and I don't think anyone else could have made that shot in quite that manner.'

'Your putt came awfully close,' another man said. 'Are you sorry it didn't drop and get you into a play-off?'

'I gave it a good roll,' she replied, 'so I'm not disappointed. Besides,' she laughed, 'the way Peggy was playing today, I can't help thinking she would have come up with something else to win, even in sudden death! I needed everything I had just to stay with her as long as I did. She deserves the win.'

Though the questions were polite, their undercurrent was obvious, and it was Ron Lieber, the least friendly of the journalists she knew, who characteristically put it into blunt words.

'A lot of people,' he said without smiling, 'wonder whether you choke in tough situations. That last putt, for instance, seemed makeable enough in the circumstances. Did you choke?'

'No,' she answered, hiding the sigh of exasperation she felt rising within her. 'I thought I stroked that putt pretty well. I wish it had gone in, but it didn't. Still, it was one of my better efforts today.'

'Nevertheless,' he pursued grimly, 'we notice a pattern in your career. You've only won three championships, and in all three cases the front-runners collapsed at the last minute to leave you in the lead. It's being said that you can't win except by default.'

Joanna shook her head with a patient smile. *Anything to get him out of my hair*, she thought privately.

'Don't count me out yet,' she said aloud. 'I've won before and I'll win again—if I play well. But I don't choke. I'm proud of my concentration and my consistency. I'll admit that it's pretty hard to win when one or another of our great players is out there having an extra special day—but that's golf for you.'

Smiles touched their knowing faces as they saw how deftly she had parried the aggressive question. Another reporter, anxious perhaps to help extricate her from Lieber's sour clutches, began asking about Pine Trail's layout and the strategy needed to play the course well. Joanna was considered the most analytical and knowledgeable of all women pros where the subtleties of golf courses were concerned, and her opinions were always eagerly sought.

The tiring interviews went on for twenty minutes before she excused herself with an apologetic smile and hurried towards the locker room. She knew Tina was waiting in Sarasota for her mother's habitual post-tournament phone call, and she intended to make it even before undressing.

She knew the room would be nearly empty, for her threesome had been the last and most of the professionals would be gone already. None of the club members had played the course today, since it was reserved for the tournament, so only an isolated tennis player might still be there, showering and changing before going up to the terrace lounge for a cocktail.

She had passed through a long corridor lined with portrait photos of the club's wealthy members, and was nearly to the locker room's heavy oak door, when a man loomed suddenly before her.

'Great tournament, Miss Lake,' he said, towering over her in the small hallway as he blocked her way. 'Sorry about the result.'

'Thank you,' said Joanna through a pained smile, moving to sidestep him. But without seeming importunate he managed to cut her off.

'I wonder if I might have a very brief word with you,' he said.

'I really must . . .' she said tiredly. 'I'm sorry, I'm in a kind of a hurry. Perhaps if you called my secretary . . .'

Perturbed by his sudden presence, she glanced quickly into his dark eyes and to the door behind him.

'I'm a great fan of yours,' he said, smiling down at her from his tall frame, 'but I'm here in a business capacity. I'm sure it will interest you. My name is Reid Armstrong.'

He extended a large hand, and reluctantly she took it.

'I'm happy to meet you,' she said, 'but as I say, I really must go now. If you'll call my . . .'

'I understand,' he said. 'But before you go, perhaps you could help me with a question—a historical question about golf. Since you're an expert on the subject, perhaps you'll know the answer.'

Joanna pursed her lips, trying to hide her irritation. *If it will make him go away*, she thought.

'How many of the championship golf courses in this country were designed by women?' he asked.

'That's easy,' Joanna laughed. 'None. All the architects were and are men. No woman has designed a tournament layout, Mr——'

'Call me Reid,' he interrupted. 'How would you like to be the first?'

Taken aback by his words, she darted a perplexed glance to his tall body and handsome face. Beneath careless waves of dark hair tinged with premature, sandy grey which gave him an oddly roguish sort of halo, he was smiling with sensual lips, his intelligent eyes riveted to her uncomfortable self. The strong lines of his tanned face suggested that he was in the prime of his thirties, all confidence and puckish humour, and quite sure of his ability to get whatever he wanted out of her.

But the irises under his dark, incisive brows were sharp and probing, and for an instant she recalled her strange impression that someone beyond the gallery and TV cameras had been watching her intently as she putted out on eighteen today.

'I don't understand,' she said, shrugging off the thought.

'I represent a group of investors who need an architect for a new course in South Carolina,' he told her. 'Beaufort County, near Hilton Head. You know the area.'

She certainly did. It was perhaps the richest single region for championship golf courses in the entire nation, and the tour had brought her there many times.

'It's simple,' he concluded bluntly. 'They want an architect. Someone excellent, someone with imagination—because they want to compete with Harbour Town and the other great courses nearby. I'm the finder they've hired, and frankly, I think you're the person for the job.'

'I . . . Mr Armstrong, I don't . . .'

'Reid,' he corrected with his inscrutable smile.

'I have no experience as an architect,' protested Joanna, unable to prevent her gaze from straying past him towards the locker room. 'I've never designed a golf hole in my life.'

'But you've thought about it, haven't you?' he said, apparently taking pleasure in hemming her in physically as well as conversationally.

She hesitated. 'Perhaps I have,' she admitted at last. 'But not in a serious, business sort of way.'

'Miss Lake,' he said, 'you shouldn't be overly modest about your abilities—or your ambitions. I'm here because I know your reputation as an analyst of golf courses, and of the game in general. I'd like you to have a look at the layout in question. It's an ocean-view situation, plenty of acreage, good soil, and lots of natural hazards. If you find it interesting, we'll talk about a commission.'

He had wasted no time in coming to the point, and he looked down at her now, his brow arched appraisingly.

'You seem to have more confidence in me than I do in myself,' she protested, glancing at her watch.

'That may well be true,' he said significantly, his gaze touched by teasing humour and by a curious, caressing glint of sympathy.

'May I ask what you mean?' she returned, irked by the impertinence of his manner.

'Look at it this way,' he said. 'If you accepted the job of architect for my people—and please understand that they fully intend to attract major championships for both men and women once the course is built—that would be an awfully ambitious project. It would make quite a name for you. It would make history, in fact. Now, unless I miss my guess, you're not the sort of woman who's comfortable with that kind of notoriety.'

'I'm not?' she repeated, bristling at his presumption.

'I think you prefer a low profile,' he explained. 'Of course, that attitude can stand in the way of legitimate ambitions, if you let it go too far. It can even prevent the development of an important talent.' His tone was cajoling.

'For a person who's never met me,' Joanna said impatiently, 'you seem to think you understand me pretty well.'

'In some ways,' he replied, 'the TV image doesn't lie. I've watched you many times. As I said, I'm a fan of yours.'

'So you did say,' she nodded, fully aware that he would not hesitate to use flattery to get what he wanted, if he thought it necessary.

'I think you're a nice person, Miss Lake,' he told her. 'Perhaps too nice. Your game is an aesthetic one. You adjust it to the specific qualities of the course you're playing. That makes you a pleasure to watch, and earns you a lot of fans. But,' he added, 'you're not the killer type, who goes out to defeat other people, and to send them home disappointed while you take the spotlight for yourself. Have I misinterpreted your screen image?'

For an instant she regarded him curiously, fascinated despite herself by the straight, hard line of his jaw and the muscular contours of his neck and shoulders. He was not only a devilishly handsome man, but appeared to be an athlete of some sort.

'Aren't you getting off the subject a bit?' she asked at length.

'Was I?' he asked, raising an eyebrow mockingly.

'Mr Armstrong,' she sighed, her patience at an end, 'I'm sorry, but I absolutely must go. Don't you think you'd better . . .'

'I'll tell you what I think,' he said more seriously. 'I think that if you took a look at the layout I have in mind, you'd find it intriguing. You'd consent to work on a tentative design for that area, and once you got started on it, you wouldn't want to stop—your natural curiosity wouldn't let you. You'd finish the design, and it would be brilliant—like everything you do in your profession. My committee would jump at the chance to build it. And the whole business would be a great step forward for women in golf.' He shrugged. 'Someone has to take that step. Why not you? You're respected and you have the ability.'

Unsettled by his unceremonious demeanour and bold proposal, Joanna returned his steady gaze with difficulty.

'And,' he added blandly, 'to be quite frank with you, the very fact that you're a woman, combined with your inexperience, will allow me to get you for this job cheaper than I could get a name male architect. That's a consideration.'

'So it's a bargain you're looking for, is it?' asked Joanna with a wry smile. 'Can't you afford a man?'

'To answer your question,' he said, 'getting you would be a great bargain indeed, Miss Lake.'

His crossed arms made the fabric of his sports coat

cling to his powerful back and shoulders as he looked down at her through dark irises in which a gleam of blue seemed to wink laughingly. She could see not only an intention to tease and to manipulate in those sharp eyes, but also a fugitive caress of genuine respect and—the thought was perplexing—pride in her.

'Correct me if I'm wrong,' she said, banishing the wave of restful warmth that had emanated from him to enfold her so suddenly. 'I imagine your investors are mostly men, and quite traditional in their outlook, like all country club people. Would it be safe to say they don't yet realise you've approached a woman with your proposition?'

He grinned. 'Your intelligence comes highly recommended,' he said. 'Yes, you're right. But I think I can guarantee you that if your work is up to your usual standards, I will be in a position to see that they accept it.'

She nodded, loath to take him at his word and yet half-convinced that he could make good on his promises.

'So you see,' he concluded triumphantly, 'with you having taken the first step, other women will follow. Less talented women, perhaps. But you'll have broken the ice.'

Joanna sighed. 'If what you say is true,' she said, 'your offer would certainly interest most of the top women pros. It might interest me. But I have to go now, Mr Armstrong . . .'

'Reid.'

'I have to go now,' she insisted, stubbornly refusing to call the stranger by a first name, 'and call my daughter.'

'Tina,' he said simply. 'She's a beautiful child—I've seen pictures of you together. She must be about to finish third grade.'

'Yes,' allowed Joanna, unnerved to hear information about her private life roll off his tongue so easily, 'she is.'

'Well,' he changed the subject with brusque assurance, 'how about dinner tonight? I'll lay out all the details for you.'

She shook her head. 'There's a dinner for Peggy tonight. I have to be there.'

'Lunch tomorrow, then?'

Again she shook her head, not quite daring to edge around him for fear that he would actually move to block her way. 'I'm driving back to Sarasota tomorrow morning,' she said. 'The next day I have to go to Orlando for another tournament. It's the beginning of the summer tour, you see . . .'

'All right, then,' he said. 'Breakfast tomorrow will be perfect. I'll meet you at your hotel. Will eight o'clock do?'

Joanna sighed, defeated. Obviously he wouldn't take no for an answer. 'Seven-thirty would be better,' she said. 'And right here on the club terrace. I'll have some last-minute business to attend to.'

'That's fine,' he smiled, extending a large tanned hand. 'You won't regret it. See you at seven-thirty, Miss Lake.'

She shook the warm, dry hand, seeing her own slender palm disappear into its caressing depths. For an instant she wondered in involuntary panic whether he would let her go. The very touch of him seemed to confirm that in his mind all obstacles must yield to his initiative, his power.

But he broke the spell with a grin. A moment later he was gone, having stood aside with a matador's grace to let her through to the locker room. Yet something of him remained around her, persistent as the smile of a Cheshire Cat, still teasing, still plying her with inscrutable charms as she hurried towards the phone.

That night Joanna spent her accustomed half-hour in the oil-scented bath which calmed her tired nerves while softening her sun-dried skin. She made it a habit to end each day of competition this way, replaying with closed eyes the eighteen holes she had faced earlier, analysing her club selections and the mechanics of her swing.

But her concentration was ceaselessly troubled by her painful knowledge that with the summer tour at its height she would see little or nothing of Tina in the two months to come. Even the sound of the little girl's bright telephone voice, already shorn of the hesitations it had borne only a year ago, made her feel lonely and anxious to hurry home tomorrow for a precious Monday together.

Her one real regret about professional golf was the gruelling summer schedule that kept her from watching the dynamic growth of Tina's tender limbs and unique personality. Karen, her long-time secretary and friend, cheerfully assumed the role of guardian in her absence, but Joanna was acutely aware that the responsibility took her away from her private life and budding career as a freelance writer.

Joanna had followed her call home with an equally traditional long-distance consultation with her college coach and mentor, Carl Jaeger.

'Jojo,' he had said, 'your round was a beauty. I'm sorry the network only covered the last five holes.'

In his gentle way he was pointing out a truth whose importance Joanna clearly saw in retrospect. She had not lost the tournament on the eighteenth hole, but much earlier, when she had inexcusably missed short putts for easy birdie opportunities on the seventh and tenth holes. She resolved to get in several hours of practice on the putting green before Thursday's opening round.

Now that Pine Trail's eighteen difficult and picturesque holes were behind her for another year,
Joanna found herself dreamily picturing their borders
of dogwood and azalea and rhododendron shrubs, and
the sycamores and black willows intentionally planted
by the architect thirty years ago to compete with the
triumphant stands of pine. He had had to plan the
entire course around the creek which wound its way
through marsh and pasture land, creating water hazards
on seven of the holes . . .

She opened her eyes suddenly, feeling the warm water
wash around her naked limbs as she started in her
surprise. She had ceased thinking as a player and was
second-guessing Pine Trail's architect.

'It's because of that man,' she told herself irritably.
'That Armstrong man. Reid . . .'

And all at once she seemed to see his rugged,
handsome face smiling down at her, goading her,
tempting her . . .

Despite his impertinence, she told herself in all
honesty, he had managed to prick her interest. If only
for the sake of women's progress in a sports world
dominated by men, a commission as architect would be
something to think about.

But she had not been deaf to the sardonic humour in
his voice. He wanted to paint a picture of her as a
woman who was afraid of her own ambition, and for
that reason alone she longed to bring him up short
somehow. If not by refusing his unlikely offer out of
hand—since she was already saddled with more than
enough obligations—then perhaps by accepting it, just
to show him she could not be so easily psychoanalysed.

The complacency in his sharp eyes came back to
taunt her. Their gaze had seemed to strip her naked, she
mused, while ironically promising only to look, and not
to touch.

Sleep did not come easily that night, and Joanna had to force herself to forget the nerve-racking aspects of the profession she loved.

'I've got to get home,' she thought before drifting off at last.

The next morning Reid Armstrong was as hard to handle as he had been in the corridor outside the locker room. Joanna arrived on the terrace to find him lounging comfortably over coffee in a pair of tight-fitting jeans which hugged his slim hips and flat stomach, and a cotton shirt open at the neck, revealing the crisp tangle of hair on his deep chest. He was the very image of lithe male confidence languid in repose.

In the morning light she noticed once more the flecks of emerald and cobalt blue which gave his dark eyes their laughing cast, and the sandy tinge lurking among the careless strands of his black hair. His long arms, uncovered on this warm morning, were obviously extremely strong.

There was something complex and multiple about his colours and his smiles, as though he was not content to remain within a single identity, like other men, but was prepared to be all things for all people. That curious ambiguity only added to his buoyant charm, for he was vibrantly compelling in his erect physical presence nevertheless.

Joanna supposed he must be an enormous success with her sex, although his mysterious, blithely knowing gaze made her conclude that he was far from her type of man. He lacked the candour and seriousness she saw as necessary attributes of the unknown man she might meet and belong to some day.

Over breakfast he repeated not only his convincing arguments in favour of her doing the course design, but also his importunate probings of her personality. He seemed to admire her precisely for the boundless ambition he thought he saw in her, and to find nothing to criticise her for except her failure to unchain that ambition entirely.

She could not recognise herself in the portrait sketched by his comments, for she considered discipline and consistency to be her best and most salient qualities. By the time they rose to leave she felt their conversation was at stalemate in every respect.

'Let me ask you something,' she sighed as they made their way among the tables towards the fragrant lawns leading to the parking lot. 'Why haven't you approached one of the big tour winners, like a Wright or a Whitworth—or a Peggy Byrne—with this proposal? Surely their names are more prestigious than mine. Wouldn't your committee find one of them a more credible choice?'

'In the first place,' he told her, 'I couldn't care less what they think. I want to find the best possible person for the job. But,' he added with his teasing look, 'before you get a swelled head, I'll tell you something else. The big winners in any sport are often not the most cerebral types. They play by instinct, and since they win, they don't spend a lot of time analysing the subtleties of their game.'

Joanna stopped short, darting him an angry gaze. 'You mean,' she asked, 'you want me because . . .'

'Because you're a loser?' he smiled. 'If the shoe fits, Miss Lake . . .'

'Thanks a lot,' she said with an incredulous shrug.

'For instance,' he explained, ignoring her pique, 'I don't imagine it's easy to beat a legend like Peggy Byrne in a big tournament like the Southern Invitation. Mentally, I mean.'

'I don't understand.'

'Well,' he went on dryly, 'she's the great popular

favourite, the winner over her illness, and she's shooting for her fiftieth win this year, isn't she? She can't very well get it if someone like you stands in her way, can she? Think how disappointed she'd be if she had to retire without reaching her goal.'

'You're very presumptuous,' observed Joanna. 'If you think I, or any other pro, would give less than a hundred per cent . . .'

'Not consciously, no,' he allowed. 'But I understand ambition, Miss Lake. Every professional athlete must have a lot of it. And he or she must be able to cope with it mentally. Ambition requires that we make other people lose, that we take the spotlight for ourselves, and refuse to share it. That's not a comfortable position for certain types of athletes.'

'And you think I'm one.' Gratefully Joanna saw her small station wagon come into view in a nearby row of cars parked on the already baking blacktop. She could hardly wait to put this arrogant man behind her.

'I'll tell you what I think,' he said, taking her bare arm in his large hand as he scanned the driveway. 'I think you're the best shotmaker in women's golf. And I think you have the best brain in the sport. However,' he went on, studying her hair and eyes with his appraising gaze, 'I suspect you need some mental training—training to win, I mean, as opposed to mere preparation for competition. Few people realise how important that is.'

'Thanks for the advice,' she cut him off, controlling her temper with an effort. 'Here's my car.'

'To get back to the business at hand,' he said, holding the door for her, 'when can I expect you in Beaufort? You'll want to see the layout.'

'I have tournaments to play,' she replied shortly. 'Perhaps after the season . . . But I'm sure you'll find someone else before then.'

'You have a break two weeks from now,' Reid pointed out calmly. 'Between the Jacksonville Pro-Am and the Eastern. You could fly down to Beaufort County at our expense and look things over. If you like what you see, you can start work next fall when the tour is over.'

'I intended to spend that week ...' she stammered, taken aback by his foreknowledge of her schedule.

'With your daughter,' he interrupted. 'Fine. She'll be out of school by then, so you can bring her along. There are lots of fun things for kids near me—and I'm sure she could use some adult male companionship.'

He had struck a nerve, and she had to fight to keep it from showing in her face.

'You don't like to take no for an answer, do you?' she asked, looking up at him from the hot driver's seat.

'No need to,' he grinned, 'when a proposal is to everyone's advantage. When will I hear from you?'

Joanne shook her head. 'I honestly don't know. Why don't you send me some sort of map of the layout, perhaps a description ...'

'It's already in the mail,' he said. 'Probably waiting for you in Sarasota.'

She raised an eyebrow. 'You're very efficient,' she commented.

'I'm paid to be,' he replied with his unflappable smile.

'And you assume an awful lot.'

'I don't think so,' he said. 'This is an opportunity—for you and for me. The job is tailor-made for you—you'll see.'

'Goodbye, then,' she said, shifting into reverse as welcome waves of cool air flowed over her bare legs from the air conditioner.

'For now,' he corrected, reaching to shake her hand. His palm was dry and protective, even in the hot morning air, and the trace of its touch remained as she turned away to grasp the wheel.

Clearly her first impression of him had not been far off, she mused as she backed the car gingerly out of its space and set off between the rows of parked vehicles. He was like the Cheshire Cat: not quite there, since one could not make him out, and yet refusing persistently to go away, his smile lingering in the air around . . .

The TV network's sound trucks, a clumsy fixture in the parking lot all week, were already gone, as were many of the cars belonging to players and journalists. The station wagon purred smoothly as its interior cooled.

Once she was on the open road the trip would be pleasant. She enjoyed driving to southern tournaments held not too far from home, for the restful ribbon of road and lovely scenery helped her to clear her mind in preparation for the next competition. Besides, the car seemed closer to Tina than the impersonal cabins of jet airliners.

At last the parking lot gave way to the smooth, tree-lined road, and Joanna pressed the accelerator. With surprising alacrity the compact wagon leapt forward.

She glanced in the rear-view mirror at the clubhouse behind which the eighteenth green, scene of her latest near-win, awaited today's round of members. Stolid as ever, the Tudor building presided over one of the most challenging courses in the South.

Before she could return her gaze to the road, a sight on the wide veranda of the clubhouse caught her eye. Outlined against the morning sky, a tall man stood alone, his arms crossed over his chest, staring straight in her direction.

It was Reid Armstrong, she realised in that split second. Even across this considerable distance which widened at every instant, he was watching her, scrutinising her, his alert gaze seeming to take in her every reaction.

He'll never give up, Joanna thought with sudden trepidation. Even in her own car, speeding homeward, she felt oddly caged, vulnerable as a fleeing prey before the quick talons of the predator.

That was the last conscious thought she was to experience for many hours.

A flash of blue seemed to overtake her from the direction of the road ahead. There was an oddly remote crunch of metal, and then a sudden twisting that gripped the car mercilessly, growing in power until it wrenched at the road, mutilated the trees and sky, tore at the sunlight, and engulfed the whole world.

Then nothing.

CHAPTER TWO

In her dream an eclipse of the sun had taken place. Night had covered everything. Blinded, she had to make believe she could see the walls and corridors of her father's house.

Dad was with her. He was pointing out a famous masterpiece hung on a wall. It was the pride of his collection. Her eyes made useless for seeing by the eclipse, Joanna began to cry. But he seemed not to notice.

How strange, she thought, that he should be blind to her blindness. But she must admit it. She must confess her shame.

Daddy, I can't see.

Meanwhile the enemy soldiers were already coming in, breaking down doors, shouting orders to each other, streaming in dark ranks around Joanna like stampeding bulls who miraculously spare the victim in their path.

Since it was wartime, all normal rules were suspended. Everything must be burnt, broken into pieces, used against the enemy or blown to smithereens before the enemy could make use of it.

Her father was nowhere to be seen now. And how terrible it was to be dressed only in her pyjamas, a pathetic little figure alone on the landing, while the troops overran everything with their fearsome shouts! In mute terror she watched, her eyes too young to show their panic.

'*Come on, little lady,*' the enemy leader said, scooping her into his arms as he beamed an amused smile down upon her. '*Show me the way.*'

His sword rattled horribly against his belt, a snakelike thing alive in its sheath. But his smile was protective, almost paternal.

'*There now*,' he laughed in triumph, swooping her higher and higher as the roar of cannon and hooves grew louder and louder, unbearably urgent and hurried, rising to a horrid peak . . .

She awoke with a wail of terror heard only as a muffled moan by the special nurse.

'Do you need something for the pain?'

At first the words sounded as foreign as the walls surrounding Joanna. Still dazed by the intensity of her nightmare, she fought to understand where she was.

The sheets were cool and comfortable. But she barely felt them, for the roar of noise inside her mind had become a climax of physical pain unlike anything she had ever experienced. Indescribably sharp and cruel, it nevertheless grew worse.

And worse.

She caught a glimpse of her leg in traction. To her right she saw the shadowy figure of a doctor hurrying into the room. Then, with all the odd naturalness of a hiccup or a sigh, something happened for the first time since her forgotten childhood. Joanna cried out aloud.

'All right, all right,' the nurse was saying. A hand patted her shoulder impotently.

'Get me a tray, Bev,' came the physician's voice. 'Let's give her a hundred milligrams of Demerol intramuscular. She has a lot of raw pain.'

Time was standing still, paralysed by unbelievable suffering, as firm hands gripped her and a tiny stab, laughably insignificant, broke the skin of her shoulder. With a strange lucidity she felt the liquid spurt from the needle's point into her flesh.

Then an enormous cottony dullness began to cover

everything, muffled and slack, suffocating and yet welcome, for it overcame everything and banished this nocturnal world of agòny and helpful, ineffectual human voices.

Am I dying? she wondered vaguely, floating into indifference. The thought would have been almost comforting in comparison with this hideous, unending victimisation that had engulfed her—had she not finally remembered who she was.

'Tina,' she moaned, unheard by the forms moving in the darkness.

Then she was asleep.

When she came to herself again a bright bar of sunlight hung across the ceiling. Its image seemed to pierce her pitilessly, fuelling what she now realised was a splitting headache behind her eyes.

Before she could close them a nurse and two doctors, alerted by the sound she must have made in awakening to her pain, converged around her.

'Joanna?' a soft voice emerged from one of the faces, soothing her with its North Carolina drawl. 'How are you feeling this afternoon? A little groggy?'

Her grimace must have told him the truth, for she saw the flash of concern in his eyes.

'Tina,' she murmured.

'Don't worry,' he said, articulating his words with exaggerated clarity, as though she were deaf. 'We're going to give you something for that pain in just a minute here. Your daughter and Karen are right outside in the corridor with Mr Armstrong. You're going to be fine. Do you understand?'

She nodded, satisfied that Tina was here. Waves of sharp pain flowed and throbbed through all her limbs, deep under her skin, as though unseen hands had cruelly toyed with her very insides during her sleep.

So I'm alive, she thought with a little pang of irony. *I can see and hear and think and feel. The better to suffer with.*

But she was grateful for life if it would allow her to be with Tina. And in her excitement she made her first mistake. She tried to move.

'No, no, no, no,' the doctor smiled indulgently as a shock of unspeakable agony smote her. 'Don't try to move. Just lie quietly and listen. Okay?'

For an answer she looked pleadingly into his grey eyes.

'My name is Dr Morrison,' he said. 'And this is Dr Diehl, from South Carolina. He's your doctor, too. You had an accident yesterday morning on the country club road. Do you remember, Joanna?'

Again she saw the mirror, the dashboard, the flash of blue against the overhanging canopy of trees, and her eyes darting an instant too late through the windshield. She nodded numbly.

'Good,' he said. 'You're a lucky young lady, Joanna. You were hit almost head-on by a fellow in a pick-up whose steering line broke. He had no control over his vehicle at all. Luckily, he's going to be all right, too.'

He had taken her hand gently. Though his touch sent new waves of pain through her, she squeezed the hand.

'All things considered,' he said, 'I think you're doing pretty well. You have a lot of bad sprains, a couple of hairline fractures in your ribs and right arm, and possibly some concussion.'

Even as he spoke the circulation of her pain began to centralise itself, and she realised what he was saving for last. The upraised knee was the focus from which her agony radiated.

The simple knowledge of it nearly made her cry out. She reached towards it stupidly, for it was in a heavy brace.

'Yes,' he nodded, stopping her hand with his own.

'You see, now, that's why we wanted to talk to you before giving you any more pain medication. The knee hurts a lot, does it?'

Joanna nodded, her lips pursed in consternation. 'Quite a lot,' she gasped, her eyes belying her measured words.

'Okay,' he said. 'That's what we need to know.' He glanced at his colleague, a younger man with greying fair hair and a droopy moustache.

'Hello, Joanna,' the man smiled, moving closer beside her. 'Can you tell me a little about the location of that pain?' He gestured without touching the knee. 'What would you say? On the outside of the knee, or the inside?'

She nodded, then shook her head in confusion.

'I . . .' she stammered. 'Inside.'

'Towards the middle, you mean. Towards the space between the legs.'

Again she shook her head, infuriated by her inability to explain herself.

'Or do you mean inside the knee itself?' he asked helpfully.

She nodded with a grateful smile.

'But not in the back of the knee,' he probed, his finger tracing an outline in the air. 'How about right behind the kneecap?'

Again she nodded, nearly terrified to hear the location of that horrid pain pinpointed so cruelly.

'All right,' he nodded. 'We're going to have to do something about that. But right now Dr Morrison will order you some medication.' Smiling under his moustache, he retreated from her field of vision, and Dr Morrison's careworn, fatherly face returned.

'Well, young lady,' he said, 'today we're going to try you on something a little more human than that Demerol. Your pain won't go away completely, but you'll be aware of what's going on around here. How does that sound?'

'Thank you, Doctor,' she said hollowly, clinging anew to the hand he proffered.

'You're going to be tired again,' he warned. 'You can see your visitors while this injection is taking effect, and then you'll have another nap—though not for thirty hours this time, I hope.'

'Is that how long ...?' She tried to touch her perspiring forehead and saw heavy tape around her right arm.

'Partially because of the Demerol,' he smiled. 'But you took quite a beating in that car of yours. Your knee hit the dash, and probably the steering column as well. The X-rays of it are clear, so we know that the problem inside is with cartilage or ligaments. I called Dr Diehl at the suggestion of Mr Armstrong—he told me he witnessed the accident.'

'Reid ...' murmured Joanna, reproaching herself too late for calling the man she barely knew by his first name.

'He's quite concerned about you,' the doctor told her. 'He's hardly left the hospital since you got here. Actually, he already knows Bob Diehl, who is, as you may know, a specialist in orthopaedics and sports medicine, and sort of got us together on this. He's a very determined man, your Mr Armstrong.' He laughed. 'I think he's even got your convalescence all planned out, as you'll soon discover.'

She nodded vaguely.

'And,' he added, 'he's been very good for Tina since she got here, if I may say so. Would you like to see her now?'

Suddenly Joanna glanced in panic at her taped limbs and bruised hands.

'What about the rest of me?' she asked. 'What do I ... look like?'

'Like what you are,' he replied seriously. 'An accident victim, Joanna. You have multiple contusions and abrasions, you're black and blue all over—but you'll be fine in time. Don't worry about Tina, she's seen you already. Children tend to accept things well. My goodness, but she's a bright little girl. The nurses have all fallen . . .'

'Can I see her now?' pleaded Joanna, unable to wait another moment.

'Sure thing,' he laughed.

A moment later Karen's freckled face and curly hair came into view. At her side was Tina, the worry in her wide eyes masked by tactful cheer.

'Mommy?' she said, patting Joanna's black-and-blue arm with a small hand. 'Mr Armstrong is going to teach me how to ride a horse!'

'Good,' Joanna sighed, too overjoyed at the sight of her daughter's face to pay much attention to her words. 'I'm sorry if I worried you,' she said, stroking the round little cheek beside which a pigtail hung fastened with rubber bands. 'Silly old Mommy managed to crack up poor Louisa.'

Tina shrugged generously at the sound of the station wagon's pet name. 'Oh, that's all right,' she said. 'Karen says we'll get a cousin of Louisa to take us around.' Behind her Karen pointed a thumb down with a grimace to indicate that the car was damaged beyond repair.

Joanna held jealously to Tina's hand as she looked at Karen. 'Is everything all right otherwise?' she asked.

'No problem,' said Karen. 'Your friend Reid is quite a guy. He's made fast friends with this one,' she glanced at Tina, 'and kept the nurses hopping! He acts like your guardian angel.'

She leaned closer as Tina watched the nurse prepare a syringe. 'It's funny,' she said, 'you'd almost think he feels responsible in some way. Anyhow, you're lucky he's been around. He called me in Florida, and helped me decide what business to do before we left, and what to bring for you. Where did you meet him?' The glimmer in her eyes bespoke her admiration for Reid's obvious charms and her assumption about the nature of his relationship with Joanna.

'Oh,' Joanna sighed, confused, 'at the club. I don't know.' Despite her concentration on Tina, the pain in her knee was becoming unbearable again, its intensity sapping her mental energies. Gratefully she felt her new injection being given.

An iridescent emptiness descended upon everything as the pain began to recede. For a long moment she kept her eyes on Tina and tried to be lucid. Surprisingly, the effort was not uncomfortable. She slipped from thought to thought as down a gentle slope leading into a propitious future.

'I'm alive,' she told herself. 'I'm still able to think, to plan, to act. I'll be able to walk out of here soon and go back to taking care of Tina.'

Then she realised with a start what had been missing in the news she had received these last few minutes.

No one had promised her that she would walk again—let alone play professional golf.

Without relinquishing her daughter's hand she let her eyes close. Instinct directed her away from panic and towards last resorts. Tina was still here, healthy and loving as always. Karen was here.

And outside somewhere, in the corridors of this hospital whose name and location she had not even thought to ask, Reid Armstrong waited.

It was called Holy Family Hospital, Joanna found out when she awoke again and began making the nurses' acquaintance. She was in Fayetteville, North Carolina, not far from Pine Trail's rustic location. Thanks to Reid's presence and quick action at the scene of her accident, she had arrived in the emergency room only twenty-five minutes after the collision.

Karen, true to form, had carefully made all the necessary arrangements both here and in Sarasota after hearing from Reid. The insurance company had been informed and the car taken to its final resting place, Joanna's twisted golf clubs and battered suitcase having been rescued from its interior. Tina's school was notified that she would be away for a couple of days. Even Joanna's winnings from the Southern Invitation had been sent to her Florida bank.

Dr Diehl was all business when he returned without his older colleague.

'I'll need you to sign this release for surgery,' he told her, placing a form on the rolling table which bore Joanna's untouched liquid breakfast. 'I want to go into that knee of yours this afternoon and see if I can't do something about your pain.'

This afternoon, she thought with a pang of dread.

'How . . . how serious is it?' she asked.

'I won't know that until I get a good look,' he said, holding out a small instrument that vaguely resembled a ballpoint pen. 'This is what I'll use, Joanna. It's called an arthroscope, and I'll be operating "through it", as we say. The incision will be small—only a couple of stitches afterwards. I won't bore you with all the anatomical details,' he smiled.

Painfully she lifted herself to her elbows so that her eyes would be somewhat at a level with his own. She was tired of being stared down at.

'I think you'd better bore me,' she said through teeth clenched by discomfort. 'My body is crucial to my profession.'

'Of course,' he said, easing her back down on the

sheets. 'Your immediate problem is what we call a
traumatic chondromalacia. Your kneecap took a hard,
direct blow, and I suspect that the cartilage behind the
kneecap is roughened as a result—possibly with a few
loose chips floating around. This is causing that intense
pain. Now, I'm going to clean up that situation with a
special tool that shaves the inside of the kneecap. It cuts
off the fragments and sucks them in, just like an electric
shaver. Meanwhile, we'll flush your knee joint with a
lot of fluid, to make sure that we get all the loose
fragments out. Although we're not scientifically positive
of this, we suspect that those little chips contain an
enzyme that can damage cartilage, so they have to go.'

He smiled encouragingly. 'That's the end of it. I think
I can promise you some good relief from the pain.'

'Will I be . . . normal, then?' asked Joanna,
determined to know the whole truth.

'Well,' he frowned, 'the chondromalacia is definite,
but I'd be less than honest if I didn't tell you that it's
probably not all you have to worry about. Your X-rays
don't show anything broken, but you may have other
problems which could be quite serious.'

'Such as?' asked Joanna, trying to hide her worry.

'Your collateral knee ligaments are probably bruised
or torn, on the inside or the outside part of the joint,'
he said, his finger pointing out the area without
touching it. 'And your lateral meniscus—that's the
cartilage that acts as a shock absorber when you work
the knee—may be damaged. If it is, it will never heal,
because cartilage happens to be about the only part of
the body that has no blood supply. We'd have to do
something about that.'

He sighed, apparently convinced that his recitation
could only bore and frighten her simultaneously, while
sounding like gibberish.

'Also,' he went on, 'you may have lost a chip or two

out of the end of the femur—the thigh bone—when the force of the accident crushed your tibia into it. We call that an osteochondritis dissecans. Then again, you might have a tear in one of the inner knee ligaments, right in the centre of the joint, between the leg bones. That's called the anterior cruciate ligament, and repairing it is no simple job. I'm going to be checking for all these things today, because none of them show up on an ordinary X-ray.'

Having absorbed this complicated vocabulary with difficulty through waves of pain, Joanna forced herself to ask the question that had tormented her for hours.

'Will I play again?''

Dr Diehl looked directly into her eyes.

'I don't know, Joanna,' he said. 'I don't know if you'll walk normally again, or run normally, or climb stairs normally, or end up with a trick knee that gives out once in a while, or a knee that hurts when it rains. There's no way to tell until we test you thoroughly. And we can't begin to do that until we get rid of that pain.'

'I see,' she said quietly. 'This afternoon . . .'

'The anaesthesia will be general,' he nodded. 'The surgery will take about forty-five minutes. I wouldn't worry about it if I were you,' he glanced at the release she had signed. 'It's not dangerous surgery in any way. But I think you should be aware that, whatever happens, you're going to need some follow-up and a lot of physical therapy. I'll need to see you at my clinic in Charleston starting Friday at the latest.'

He smiled. 'That's where Reid Armstrong comes in. He lives not thirty miles from our clinic, and he tells me he's all set to put you up, and Tina as well when she finishes school, while you convalesce. Personally, I think it's a good idea. The clinic is basically an out-patient operation, and it would be very boring for you to stay there.'

Struggling to take all these facts in, Joanna looked up at him.

'Reid Armstrong?' she queried. 'I barely . . .'

'Another advantage he'll offer you,' he went on, 'is that he knows my methods. I helped him out once, years ago, when he was injured playing college football. You're going to need a whirlpool and some Nautilus equipment, and he's already arranged to have it installed, I believe. A friend in need, as they say . . .'

Joanna could only nod helpless acquiescence. Unnerved by the thought that she might be irreparably damaged in some way, she could not deal with his bewildering revelations.

A moment later he was gone. Lying alone in the room, she stared at the ceiling, assailed by irrational fears.

Surgery.

The word terrified her. She had never been in a hospital as a patient in her life. She had never injured herself in a sports career that already spanned more than a decade. A bad attack of 'flu was the worst ailment she had ever suffered.

She could not force from her mind the stories she had heard about the dangers of anaesthesia. That, no doubt, was the chief concern behind the release Dr Diehl had made her sign.

Silly, she reproached herself. *That's about as likely as getting hit by a . . .*

Then she remembered. She *had* been hit by a truck, when she least expected it. The unlikely could and did happen.

She sighed in consternation. Normal life seemed so remote now, exiled by this artificial reality of pain, fear, and drugged apathy. And Dr Diehl steadfastly refused to promise that one day she might be herself again.

The five hours before surgery would have been

unbearable had it not been for Reid and Tina, who entered the room not long after Dr Diehl's departure. His large hand on the little girl's shoulder, Reid dwarfed her strikingly. Yet she seemed at home in the shadow of his huge, smiling form, and sat in his lap complacently when she was not wandering the room or holding Joanna's hand.

'You're big news already,' he said, showing her the latest issue of *Sports Illustrated*, whose editors had managed to include a small note about her accident after their account of her loss to Peggy at Pine Trail.

'Karen has all the newspapers,' he added. 'Your face is all over the sports pages. Looks like injury is better publicity for you than winning!'

'Very funny,' sighed Joanna, grateful for his levity even though she could not for the life of her understand what he was doing here.

'Tell me,' he asked Tina, 'what do you think of your mom today?'

'Mm-m,' the child hesitated, twisting on his lap, 'same as always, I guess. She's a little black and blue, of course, but that's to be expected in the circumstances.'

Joanna had to smile at Tina's precocious language. Reid merely nodded in silent agreement, neither patronising her nor hiding his amusement.

'Which is worse?' he asked. 'Her contusions or her confusion?'

'What are you talking about?' Joanna erupted from her bed. 'Drugs or no drugs, I've never been more clear-headed in my life!'

'Good,' he drawled. 'That means you can start making plans for your convalescence at my place.'

Joanna shook her head, too emotionally exhausted to start a lengthy argument with him. It was impossible to comprehend that this total stranger had somehow managed to choose her doctor, to determine the site of

her recovery, and even to befriend her daughter. Yet it
was Reid who had called the ambulance for her, Reid
who had called Karen—and now Joanna could even
recall having read or heard from other athletes about
Robert Diehl's fame as a sports specialist.

Everywhere she looked in her jumbled life, it seemed,
Reid had suddenly managed to leave his mark. From
the moment he had loomed up in front of her in the
portrait-lined corridor at Pine Trail, it had been
impossible to get rid of him. Circumstances had added
themselves to his natural persistence, so that now he
had become a virtual fixture in her existence, at once
indispensable and unfamiliar.

Who could tell, she wondered, what others must
think of her relationship with him, since he had been
haunting these hospital corridors so loyally? What must
Dr Diehl think? And Tina . . .

And, if the truth be known, she reflected uncomfortably, Reid had even played a part in causing the
accident itself. Of course, she would never be able to
admit that embarrassing fact to anyone—much less to
Reid himself. But she could not wipe it from her
memory. Even as a small figure in her rear-view
mirror, Reid had managed to fascinate her sufficiently
to distract her from the road ahead.

And, as luck would have it, that single instant had
been the crucial one.

No, she thought ashamedly. No one must ever know
of her foolishness or her chagrin.

And yet Reid seemed to know or suspect the truth
of the situation. Even Karen had felt his sense of
responsibility in his overwhelmingly scrupulous presence here, his protectiveness as Joanna's 'guardian
angel' . . .

She blushed to think that she and Reid shared this
most intimate secret, despite the fact that they were still

perfect strangers. A secret that they could never confide to anyone else—or to each other.

It was all too much, she thought resignedly. Some day, when this mess was behind her, she would be on her own and self-determining again. But for the moment she was helpless and frightened, and she could not disdain the confident humour with which Reid kept her from dwelling on the surgery to come.

And he was unfailingly cheerful, teasing her unmercifully as he watched Tina's peregrinations about the room or held her in his lap.

'When you think of it,' he said blandly, 'things always have a bright side. While you're at my place there won't be much to amuse you, so you'll have time on your hands. I'll show you the Black Woods layout and maps, and you can give some serious thought to the design, maybe even plan a few holes right away. I know you'll fall in love with the place. And, if you're as lucid as you say you are, I won't hesitate to expect great things from you.'

Joanna had forgotten all about the proposal which was at the source of her misfortune.

'Honestly,' she groaned, 'you are the most presumptuous man I've ever met in my life! You've got me up to my neck in your own plans, and I don't even know if . . .'

He looked over Tina's shoulder at Joanna, his dark eyes alert as those of a jungle cat. The child, absorbed in the book she had brought, did not see the intensity that quickened in his irises.

'If you'll walk out of here?' he asked, reading Joanna's fears easily. 'I'll tell you something, Miss Lake. You'll not only walk out of here—on crutches at first, I'll admit—but you'll play golf again, and you'll win. I intend to see to it. And I don't like to take no for an answer.'

His gaze softened. 'And,' he added, 'you're going to be the first woman to design a top-twenty championship course. I want it to be a difficult test, you know, so that when you play it on the tour you won't have an unfair advantage as the architect.'

'For heaven's sake,' she sighed, hiding her gratitude for his confidence, 'you might as well call me Joanna.'

'All right,' he said, patting Tina's shoulders. 'And you can call me any names you like—as soon as you're back in top shape.'

As the minutes stretched languidly into hours, Joanna watched the interplay between Reid and Tina from her propped-up position in bed. It was more than obvious that he had easily won the child's friendship and trust—probably during the nocturnal hours when his reassurance and distracting presence prevented her from worrying that her mother would die from the accident.

Yes, Joanna mused as she watched their quiet laughter and conversation. They had the air of two people who have been through something painful together. Something that has brought them closer.

Yet all the while she could not help noticing his enormous male vitality, coiled in that small chair across the room, sending its waves of silent urgency in her direction, unbeknownst to her oblivious daughter.

Or were the drugs and the pain playing tricks on her again? She could not tell. In his gentle humour and unflappable confidence there was a virility that charged the air around him, forcing her into acute awareness of him as a man at every instant. Despite herself she blushed to think he was seeing her in her battered condition.

Even as she reflected on these ideas, the medication for her pain was wearing off in preparation for the general anaesthesia which must come this afternoon. As the hour drew nearer for fearsome oblivion, her thoughts became more coloured by her nagging discomfort, and it seemed that her emotions were in as bad a mess as her body.

She was angry at Reid for his brusque, manipulative invasion of her private life—and grateful to him for his help. His irritating certainty that she would eventually do his bidding seemed unforgivable; yet there was nothing so unreasonable about what he had asked.

Fate seemed to conspire with him at every turn. In his arrogance he had promised Tina he would teach her how to ride a horse. Yet, in all likelihood, he had calculated the probabilities beforehand and knew he would be in a position to make good on his promise.

With a pang she thought how quickly Tina had attached herself to the first truly male figure she had been close to in her young life.

'Well,' she sighed inwardly, 'I suppose it's better to have him on my side than against me. At least he's more encouraging than Dr Diehl!'

Now the pain was radiating in a weird symphony from her knee to all the corners of her body. Clear thinking was no longer possible. She was almost grateful when the nurse came with a tray for her preparatory injection.

Let's get it over with, she thought grimly as the needle punctured her. Let Dr Diehl use all his skill and heroism if necessary. Anything to deaden this awful, angry pain!

'You'll feel a little sleepy now,' said the nurse in a hurried but amiable voice. 'The orderlies will bring a table in a moment to take you to the operating room.'

Sleepy? Joanna thought. *Dopey is more like it.* The words were taking on an antic absurdity as the powerful drug overwhelmed her senses.

Sleepy, Dopey, Grumpy, Bashful . . .

She thought she was laughing at the silliness of everything around and inside her. But already she was being wheeled under the corridor's painted ceiling, doing her best to respond to the orderly's pleasant question about golf. But the simplest words would not come. She found herself unable to make her mouth move properly.

Then there were doctors around her. She heard Robert Diehl's voice, harsher and more authoritative now. The anaesthesiologist, a kindly, bespectacled man, forced a needle into her vein and sat beside her, his smile vanishing as he said, 'She's ready, Doctor.'

Horrified to be capable of thought just as her body was to be invaded by foreign instruments, Joanna fought to help her mind wander away.

In time she would see to everything, she resolved. She would make decisions, take command of things, take care of Tina. When she was on her feet again. She was accustomed to being in charge of her little family, and nothing would change that—Reid Armstrong notwithstanding.

But for now she must withdraw from this reality of pain and dread.

So she let herself slip into the past, numbed by the brutal anaesthetic. She saw herself seated as Tina had been, comfortable and complacent, on the secure and unmoving lap of a man as steadfast as an edifice, on a hot summer evening in a small Southern town, on a porch beside a quiet street, long ago, long before the busy, hurried years that had led to this moment of truth.

CHAPTER THREE

'Scoot over an inch, honey—these old legs of mine are going to fall asleep in another minute.'

Paul Lake's voice, its lilting drawl as rhythmic as the swaying old couch on which he sat in the shadows, was the sleepy destination of each sunlit day, and its sweetest moment for Joanna.

She could feel him nod approval as she recounted her doings at school or at play in the neighbourhood. Absently he patted her shoulder, acknowledging her childish words with little murmured responses, alert to the muted sounds from inside the house where Ellen was seeing to Chris, and yet all grave attention to Joanna.

She was eight years old, and if she had a care in the world, it was always banished by this lulling, whispered hour in the cradle of her father's arms. The sound and touch of him were as permanent and warmly dependable as the crickets under the porch, the katydids falling silent in the trees, and the neighbours who passed by on Grandview Street with a wave and a smile.

So secure was that nightly moment, stretching before her in its lazy perfection, that she tried her best to make it last. But it was, after all, the end of the day, as Paul always seemed to know before she did.

'Upsy-Daisy,' he would croon as he raised her to his own great height, the front lawn wheeling past her half-closed eyes as the screen door swung open. 'That's my girl!'

And she would be asleep before he placed her softly on her bed—and only half-wakened when Ellen came up to kiss her.

So that, in a way, the languid moment on the porch had never ended, but had gently closed her eyes to what came after.

She had been born in Atlanta, where the steel and granite towers Paul helped build with his construction crews stood as shining symbols of the New South.

But she had spent her first years in the tiny town of Crane, twenty-five miles away. And it was there that she put down her emotional roots, her ears filled with names like Macon, Albany and Savannah, her field of adventure encompassing all the dark corners of the venerable but rickety house that Paul had bought for his new family.

Like the porch's swinging couch, whose occasional whines of old age lent the still night air some of its charm, the house came to bear innumerable traces of Paul's patient, stubborn repairs. Piqued in his engineer's mind by the challenge of outwitting inevitable decay, he liked to amuse himself by fixing the most unsteady of its ancient trappings, rather than to replace them with something more seemly.

Having long since learned to cease protesting his heroic labours in the name of common sense, Ellen would watch him with lips pursed in a half-smile of resignation, and then turn back to her own housework, tossing her curly hair over a tired shoulder as the smile's ghost lingered in her busy eyes.

Paul's aura of quiet calm, incarnated for Joanna in the warm lap and long arms whose embrace was firm and comforting as the ground under one's feet, seemed to be his particular and irreplaceable essence. It pervaded even the moments when he had to discipline her or Chris, the vibrant little sister born three years after her. Though Joanna could not understand at the time, it was also a crucial balance in his loving marriage to Ellen, a far more volatile personality than he.

Everyone said that little Joanna, with her grave eyes and thoughtful demeanour, took after Paul, while bustling, excitable Chris was her mother's daughter. And even that familiar pronouncement, spoken now by a red-faced uncle, now by a smiling grandparent, seemed a faithful friend, a pleasant landmark of life on peaceful Grandview Street.

Joanna felt privileged to be likened to the tall, reflective man whose inner serenity seemed obscurely linked to his power over objects. It was Paul who restored things and made them permanent, no matter what the damage wrought by accident or the passage of time. Thanks to Paul, what was old could also be what lasted.

Years later, when she realised how deeply she had come to love her South for the endurance which which it hid and protected its gentle roots even as harsh decades of change overtook it, her wistful thoughts would turn to Paul.

For in her life he had been the slow and comforting passage of days, each one as perfect and familiar as the last, their stately rhythm providing a wide-eyed little girl with the sense of security her growth required, while exposing her unfortunately and inevitably to the lulling illusion that some things are permanent.

One day she came home from third grade to find a police car parked in front of the old house. Inside, two officers sat uncomfortably on the living room couch, their black uniforms sending cold tendrils of strangeness into all the corners. Ellen was seated as far from them as possible, five-year-old Chris on her lap. She seemed to have recoiled from them in panic, as from their news. Her tear-stained eyes shot to Joanna with an odd look, angry and pleading and perhaps resigned, which passed unnoticed by the others.

Joanna knew before she had to be told. Paul was dead.

He had been killed in a scaffold accident high above the site on which his men were working. His last breaths were drawn in the emergency room of an Atlanta hospital, far from his home and family. There had not been time to inform Ellen until he was already gone.

With the quick adaptability of childhood Joanna survived her loss. In her mind Paul was a shade now, a presence in every warm Georgia night. In fact, he was as much part of the night's quiet essence as of the old house's dignity. So convinced was she of his continuing influence over her life that she viewed Ellen's cold grief with puzzlement.

She never forgot that brittle, pleading look that Ellen had flashed her in the presence of the officers. Whether it carried a weight of responsibility or not, somewhere inside her child's heart Joanna decided that she must serve as a living link not only between Paul and his widow, but between Ellen and little Chris, who risked growing up without ever experiencing the warm security Joanna herself had taken for granted.

Joanna was the lucky one, the first-born child for whom Paul had lived too intensely to be eliminated by death. Therefore, she reasoned, she must help those who had lost him.

So it was that, when Ellen found full-time work, Joanna became adept at helping to prepare dinner and clean the house. Before long she was attending Chris's school plays, walking with her to the dentist or pediatrician on Main Street, reading her school reports and the childish stories she wrote, and generally assuming a maternal role which the three-year gap between the sisters would never have justified otherwise.

A year after Paul's death Ellen sold the house and moved her family to a comfortable but nondescript apartment. Unseen and unfelt by anyone, Paul Lake took up a position deeper inside Joanna's soul, secure and invisible to outsiders, now that his beloved house was gone.

And life went on as grade school gave way to junior high. Ellen worked hard, with a stolid, somewhat harsh gaiety, while slim, reflective Joanna devoted herself to Chris, who grew more spunky and vital each year.

Joanna found herself inexplicably popular at school. She was in the chorus, on the debating team, and was voted Most Intelligent in her class. Everyone admired her and came to her when in need of advice. It was assumed she would go to college and become a professor or lawyer or doctor.

She alone never questioned her certainty that she would one day become an engineer.

But again the gentle sequence of days passing one like another showed its fragility.

On a windswept day in March, when she was in eighth grade, Joanna was asked by a classmate to join her for a round of golf.

The girl was Sissy Macomber, the daughter of an extremely rich and respected family. Having set her sights on making friends with her popular classmate, Sissy cheerfully showed Joanna around the Country Club's fabulous oak hallways lined with studio portraits of the prosperous men who were its members.

The girls sneaked into a huge lounge filled with overstuffed chairs, and purloined a few delicious-looking peanuts from wooden bowls in the empty bar. After their round of golf they ate hamburgers in the dining room and bowled a game in the small alley beneath the members' steam rooms and squash courts.

Joanna decided she had not had so carefree and amusing a day in a long while. A trifle jealous of Sissy's heedless enjoyment of such money and luxury, she went home to prepare dinner as usual.

But her frail fourteen-year-old presence had made its impression at Fairhaven Golf and Country Club.

Juan, the caddy who accompanied the girls on their somewhat giggly eighteen-hole outing, saw Joanna miss the ball completely on her first swing. The patient pro shop assistant explained to her the virtues of keeping one's eye on the ball, and on her next swing Joanna obediently hit a vicious slice that screamed far out of bounds.

But Juan noticed with his practised eye that the ball had flown at least one-hundred and seventy-five yards in the air.

By the end of the round he could hardly wait to tell his fellow caddies what he had seen. Correcting her mistakes with uncanny instinct, Sissy's young guest had improved dramatically with each hole she played, and had actually finished the back nine in fifty strokes. Such a performance from a pure novice was unheard-of.

Word soon reached Ralph Kohler, the club professional, who related it to Mrs Macomber. That lady, determined to cement her daughter's new friendship, spoke with Ellen Lake on the phone before inviting Joanna to join Sissy for another round.

A week later Ellen informed Joanna that she might play golf every day throughout the summer, since an arrangement had been made with some neighbours to watch out for eleven-year-old Chris.

Somehow Joanna never thought to ask why her golfing friendship with Sissy had become so time-consuming, or why she found herself receiving regular lessons from Ralph Kohler. She contented herself with the dozens of Cokes, bags of potato chips, hamburgers, and conversations about boys that made up her days with the gregarious Sissy.

Ralph Kohler realised that in Joanna he had found a once-in-a-lifetime pupil. Thanks to her perfect instinctive concentration and natural inclination towards neatness and correctness, she could play a casual round punctuated by laughing byplay with Sissy—and all the while refine her talent, perfect her swing, choose her shots with ever-increasing intelligence and foresight.

By summer's end the club teemed with whispers about Ralph's prodigy. Joanna was still only five feet tall and weighed eighty-seven pounds, but the gentle curves of her shoulders and thighs concealed fine muscles, and her every move was so filled with fluid rhythm that she already seemed a young champion. Her game was approaching competitive quality with a rapidity that left witnesses breathless.

But Ralph bided his time. He knew that golf was just a game to Joanna, so he treated it as such. He rewarded her progress with sodas and ice cream cones, kept Sissy near her, and made her play catch with the caddies, watching her carefree animal grace in admiration from a distance. When he met Ellen he tried to imagine the tricks of heredity that had produced a young miracle like Joanna. But Ellen was not particularly athletic— and the girl's father was dead.

Golf became a fact of life for Joanna. She never gave a thought to what she was doing, even when her training extended through most of the winter, taking up more hours each day, even when she had to learn to budget her time in order to finish her schoolwork.

Sometimes she would return home to find Ellen reading to Chris or teaching her to sew. And now Chris was old enough to help with dinner. Grateful for each smile she saw them exchange, Joanna felt both relieved that they got along so well together, and a trifle jealous of this closeness from which she was so often excluded nowadays.

The next summer Ralph entered Joanna in the Western Junior Girls' Championship, which she won easily, defeating competitors who had been brought along for seven to ten years by their own club pros or hired teachers. Her performance passed as a fluke among the alert observers who knew how little experience she had.

But when she won the U.S.G.A. Girls' Junior Championship the same summer, her anonymity became a thing of the past, as did the playful aspect of her golfing experience. Besieged by eager reporters who asked her everything from the mechanics of her game to her opinion on world events, she could only answer in abashed, graceless monosyllables. Yet her innate seriousness as an individual charmed the press, and the seeds of her future popularity were sown.

By the time she won the Georgia Amateur Championship at the age of sixteen, Joanna was finding golf a burden. The subtle pressure she felt from all sides to continue time-consuming competition made her feel cramped and conspicuous at school. Though a confident champion on the golf course, she remained a gangly, frightened adolescent inside her emotions. Golf was tearing at her and losing its appeal.

She solved this problem by playing each round, each tournament in a sort of controlled trance. Her mind far away in reveries about the handsomest boy in the junior class, she let her body solve its own problems on the course. Ignoring her competition, she let herself float among the girlish fantasies that came naturally to her.

Without realising it Joanna had discovered a secret known only to the greatest of athletes. By keeping her inner mind off the demands of her game, she freed the secret mentality of her nerves and muscles to function without stress. She played her best through the simple fact of not forcing her shots. By taking the pressure off herself she became a pure athlete.

By the middle of her junior year she had won amateur championships all over the south. Admiring articles about her flawless swing, shotmaking imagination and amazing consistency had appeared in all the golf magazines.

Yet now her thoughts were further from golf than ever. It was time to think about college. But Ellen's hard-earned savings were laughably inadequate for such an idea.

And only now Joanna began to speculate uncomfortably on how much Ellen might have spent on her three years of golf training and competition. She cursed the distracting hobby that had blinded her to her responsibility to her family, even as it had made her miss so many happy, ordinary days with Ellen and Chris these past years. Days that were as remote now as her chances of becoming an engineer.

But all at once the silver lining of those bumpy adolescent years showed itself, and colleges and universities from all over the United States offered Joanna complete golf scholarships.

Infinitely relieved not to have to be a burden on Ellen, Joanna at last saw some usefulness in her talent for golf. She accepted the offer from the University of Georgia in Athens—not only because of its warm southern location, propitious for golf in winter, but also because it was in her beloved state and near her mother and sister.

At first the university was unfamiliar and scary. The dorms were filled with strange, confident young women who seemed not to share Joanna's fear of the abrupt and demanding professors. But Joanna applied herself, forcing back her feelings of distress, and made good grades.

The intercollegiate golf competitions she participated in seemed at once to separate her from her peers and to swallow up her free time. Were it not for Carl Jaeger, her coach at Georgia and a champion as a professional three decades earlier, Joanna would have grown to hate the game that was now a necessity for her scholarship.

Carl became a virtual father to her during their first season together. Having taken an immediate liking to the quiet, serious girl who could beat his best male players, he set out to refine her natural ability while making her feel more comfortable on the course.

Pricking her instinctive engineer's wit and curiosity, Carl taught Joanna to appreciate the intellectual challenge of golf's chesslike complexity, and to perfect clever shots which other players lacked the imagination to conceive.

Astonished by his pupil's uncanny grasp of subtleties it had taken him twenty years to learn, Carl began to believe that with proper training she might find a place for herself in the amateur record books, and his conviction was hardly shaken when, in her first year with him, Joanna won the Women's Southern Amateur, placed second in the Women's South Atlantic Golf Tournament, and helped her team to victory in the Women's World Amateur Team Championships.

At eighteen Joanna was not only an intercollegiate celebrity, but was one of the most highly regarded amateur players in the world. But unbeknown to her legions of unseen fans, she was one of the loneliest college sophomores in the country.

She could not seem to get used to life without Chris and Ellen. Her golfing journeys to unfamiliar places only exaggerated her sense of exile in a coldly competitive world which must soon separate her for ever from the home she loved. Though her engineering major stimulated and distracted her, she knew that it, also, was leading inevitably into a solitary future. Each time she went home on vacation she felt like a stranger in the apartment whose daily routine she no longer shared.

Her adolescent shape had given way to a lithe, willowy figure which attracted the opposite sex perhaps more than she would have liked. Yet the college men she met seemed immature and flighty. And she suspected that they feared her somehow—not only because she was an athlete, and a famous one to boot, but also because there was a fundamental seriousness about her, inherited from Paul, that harmonised badly with their impulsive ways.

Tormented now by guilt over the expense of her amateur career, she longed to graduate and find work as an engineer. But two more years of school stood between her and a field whose storied opportunities were already being diminished by the near-collapse of the space programme. Meanwhile, she knew it was time for Chris to begin thinking about college, and for Ellen to wonder where her younger daughter's tuition money must come from.

Joanna was at sixes and sevens. An unbearably depressing emptiness had descended over her life, and she could not see a way into the future.

She met Jack Templeton when she was in this painful state. And Jack seemed tailor-made to pluck her out of it.

He belonged to an old-established family whose ancestors included two Civil War generals, and whose enormous wealth was traceable not only to the Old South's confluence of cotton and tobacco farming, but also, it was rumoured, to the exploits of the arrogant buccaneers who had once plundered its coastal waters.

Joanna had met him, predictably enough, on the golf course. An avid golfer, like generations of his family's men before him, he played a scratch game and had been on the golf team for two semesters before his studies and fraternity obligations forced him to quit.

When Jack found that he could not beat Joanna, despite his superior strength off the tee, he applauded her excellence without a trace of ill-humour and immediately placed her on a pedestal for her bright personality as well as her athletic skill.

For her own part, Joanna could not be blind to her new friend's extraordinary charms. A tall, lean man in his senior year, Jack glowed with the easy confidence Joanna lacked so sorely. With his curly black hair and aquiline nose, his square shoulders and long, striding legs, he cut a dashing figure. Though one sensed generations of breeding in his gentility and impeccable manners, he bore his ancestry with carefree negligence.

His intense and even hawklike look, dark eyes flashing with quick wit and intelligence, fascinated Joanna most of all. He intended to seek a career in government service after completing his political science degree, and he made no secret of his healthy contempt for his family's reactionary attitudes. Yet in his very independence of mind, so roguish and devil-may-care, he seemed outlined against the colourful background of his adventurous forebears.

Soon he invited Joanna to dinner, to the movies, and to do her studies with him. He asked her to join him with his parents when they visited Athens, and squired her through the rather uncomfortable occasion without a false step, keeping his dour father at bay with sparkling humour while showering his mother, a quiet and seemingly defenceless little woman, with a son's easy affection.

Jack made no secret of his admiration for Joanna, or,

as time went on, his desire for her. The touch of his warm hands on her shoulders gave way at last to caressing embraces, his friendly kisses to more passionate, probing ones. And Joanna realised all at once that she was seriously involved with him.

Her thought must have communicated itself in the gravity of her limpid green irises, for he smiled, took her hand and, as easily as he had so often carried her golf bag or held a car door open for her, proposed marriage.

'In the first place,' he said, 'I can't live without you, Joanna. In the second place, my family is afraid of you. And in the third place, you're the only girl I've ever met who can destroy me on the golf course. I see a lifetime of defeats ahead of me. Won't you make it a reality?'

In the laughing glitter of his dark eyes there was respect, deference, and the vulnerability of a young man in search of his own future—as well as the fugitive trace of the romantic buccaneer who swears undying allegiance to his lady. He was an exalted lineage made solid and handsomely human—and he wanted Joanna.

Suddenly it seemed that her continuing education, her uncertain career, his own future struggles, and her sense of responsibility to Ellen and Chris, must all yield to the great sigh of relief brought by that simple, infinitely welcome fact. He wanted her.

With one word she could put an end to her floundering solitude. Life as Joanna Templeton spread before her, a sane, regular vista, just as in her childhood she had imagined the stately world of adults to be.

She said yes.

She was to recognise her error an instant too late.

The wedding was held the day after Jack's graduation in a small church near Ellen's apartment in Crane. Jack's parents were there alone, without the hundreds of Templeton relatives who undoubtedly had expected to attend. Jack had had his way in ensuring Joanna the quiet wedding he knew she wanted.

But the look in Ellen's hazel eyes was worried that day. Catching a glimpse of it in a mirror from across the room, Joanna thought she recognised it. Ellen was responding uncomfortably to the Templetons' small talk, her arm curled tightly around Chris's shoulder, as though to hold her close and protect her from a fate still unseen by anyone but Ellen herself.

All at once Joanna remembered. It was that secret look, filled with harsh resignation, that Ellen had shot her way in the presence of the two policemen the day of Paul's death. But now it was a private shadow in Ellen's features, hidden from Joanna herself.

As usual, Ellen's simple, acute intelligence was clairvoyant. Within days after her marriage Joanna began to suspect that something was wrong.

Jack decided to go to work for his father's investment firm after all, now that he had graduated, and to postpone his career in public service until he was settled and had made some contacts around the state. He and Joanna moved into an attractive Savannah apartment, with the unspoken understanding that after a suitable interval they would start looking for an appropriate house.

Jack's accustomed smiles grew less and less frequent when he returned from work. Joanna began to notice a look of stubborn recalcitrance under his dark brow when a subject came up that challenged certain ideas he held dear—ideas to which he had been happily indifferent only weeks or months before.

His sense of humour seemed more brittle, more sardonic now, and was turned with surprising venom on people and things he had fancied in earlier times. And it was never, never directed at himself or his family, as it had been when she first knew him.

Puzzled by the surprising change that had come over him almost overnight, Joanna supposed the sudden pressure of marriage and a necessary livelihood were taking their toll on his nerves. But when her tender solicitude only succeeded in making him more sullen and moody, she suspected a deeper trouble.

Jack simply was not himself any more. A dour heaviness seemed to have overtaken him, banishing his youthful vivacity. She noticed not only his family resemblance to his staid father Charles, but also an almost unwitting style of carriage, a way of picking up a cup of coffee or entering a room, a turn of phrase, which imitated the older man disturbingly.

Peering intently at herself in the mirror, Joanna wondered whether she was suffering from some sort of hallucination. The kind young man she had married was gone, and in his place was a stranger who behaved as though he had been hurt or cheated in some way, and who obviously blamed Joanna for being unwilling or unable to make things right. To make his reproach crystal clear he rejected her attempts at affectionate reconciliation with harsh, dismissing words.

When she finally bristled at the thankless nursemaid role he expected her to play, he became abusive, accusing her of slights and betrayals so subtle that it was impossible to be sure from his twisted smile whether he was serious or, in some sick way, joking.

For weeks she was amazed and tied up in knots by the strange guilt he seemed bent on attibuting to her. Then all at once she realised the truth.

Jack's whole courtship had been a charade. He had never intended pursuing an independent life with Joanna. His marriage meant the opposite to him; it signified his coming of age and inevitable surrender to his family's domination. That was why he had brought his new wife straight to Savannah and gone to work for his father. He would never seek appointive or elective political office unless it was under the aegis of his family or their friends.

Jack had chosen a life of dependence in which he could never compete as a man with the father he feared. And he blamed Joanna for his own weakness—and always would.

The revelation was so stunning in Joanna's mind that she could not believe it at first. But it made so much sense, and explained so much that she had seen and heard in the Templeton family, that she could doubt it no longer.

She contemplated silent, helpless Flora Templeton, who had spent a lifetime fluttering about the rooms of her wilful husband's huge old house, and was now incapable of a single independent thought or act.

Is that what I have to look forward to? Joanna wondered, seeing herself mirrored in Jack's grim, reproachful eyes—and she already knew she was not going to wait around to find out.

She was on the point of broaching the subject of separation when, three months after her wedding, she was told she was pregnant.

It was a pivotal moment for Joanna. Though tempted to cling to her painful marriage in order to ensure some sort of security for her unborn child, she knew that a childhood in Jack's family could be nothing but madly insecure. The fearful thoughts about Ellen and Chris that had haunted her before her marriage were forgotten now. Sanity and happiness were too valuable to be sacrificed to mere financial survival.

She decided to renounce her personal failure before the child was born, and leave Jack to the life he had chosen for himself.

To her surprise, Jack docilely agreed. Apparently

aware that Joanna was his match in will and stubbornness, he was more than willing to seek a more pliant mate elsewhere.

Their divorce was made final a week before Joanna completed her solitary junior year at Georgia—and a month before Christina Lake, named for Joanna's own sister, was born.

Taking a deep breath, Joanna resolved not to accept child support from the Templetons; she did not want Jack to feel either an obligation or a parental privilege towards the child he had sired almost by accident.

She applied for a renewal of her golf scholarship effective after her baby's birth, but was told that all athletic scholarships were expressly forbidden to women who became pregnant. So she took out a university loan for tuition, bravely borrowed money from Ellen for books, found a furnished room in Athens for herself and her baby, and brushed up on her already speedy typing. She would type dissertations and course papers to support herself until she graduated.

On a hot June morning she entered the County Hospital near Crane and had her baby. Her labour seemed short and almost painless, but when it was over she was surprised to hear Ellen say it had lasted nine hours.

She could not take her eyes off the baby. A creature of indescribable beauty, Tina was utterly individual. She resembled neither Joanna nor Jack, nor any of the Templetons or Lakes; she was her own unique little person.

On her return to Athens Joanna saw an item in the social column announcing the engagement of Jack Templeton to the youngest daughter of a Savannah family nearly as wealthy as his own. The two families were joined by financial ties going back for generations.

Joanna laughed and danced around her furnished

room with Tina in her arms. She was truly free at last from the marriage that had threatened to ruin her life. Jack was safe in his own future, and in her arms she held the greatest gift he could have left her.

Her marriage had lasted less than a year. Now she was out in the real world, and glad to be there. Its fresh air more than compensated for its dangers and challenges.

Oddly enough, Joanna thought with a rueful smile, Jack had never made good his promise. Not once after their marriage had he joined her on the golf course. Though he did not ask her to give up her golf—reasoning, no doubt, that her fame distinguished him in his family while falling nicely into the category of amateur talents for females, such as piano playing or landscape painting—he had played exclusively with his old fraternity brothers or newfound business associates.

But her smile was forced, for her own days as a golfer were over. Golf could no longer help her through school. Engineering must now absorb her thoughts.

Thanks to her midnight struggles with quantum mechanics and high-energy physics during Tina's sleep, Joanna made the Dean's List midway through her senior year.

Two months before the graduation for which she had worked so hard, she was interviewed by visiting recruiters from corporations representing the spectrum of engineering opportunities nationwide. To a man they looked askance at her divorce and the fact that she was the sole support of her daughter.

'If we hire a man,' she was told, 'he'll stick with us, and go where we tell him to go. But what if you remarry, Miss Lake? What if you have a second child? What if your next husband gets transferred? All the time and money we'll have spent in training you would be wasted. If times were easier, things would be different . . .'

To her horror Joanna saw her engineering diploma for what it was: a frail piece of paper barely adequate to assure her the lowest-paying of jobs.

For Ellen's sake she went through her bitter graduation ceremony, returned her cap and gown and put her diploma in the closet of her furnished room in Athens. Her four years of college were all but useless to her. She had no earning power, and a child to support.

For the third time in her life Joanna was totally at sea.

Karen Gillespie, the vivacious and hardheaded former college room-mate Joanna had hired to babysit for Tina when classes kept her away from the room, came to her rescue with a careless shrug.

'Turn pro,' she advised. 'Go on the L.P.G.A. tour.'

Thunderstruck, Joanna objected that she had not touched a golf club in over a year.

'Look, Joanna,' said Karen, 'you were a great amateur champion. I know you as well as I know myself. You've got good nerves and you don't get discouraged when things don't go your way—unless I miss my guess, those are exactly the qualities a professional athlete needs.'

Carl Jaeger disagreed vehemently when Joanna went to see him. The women's tour, he said, was just as gruelling as the men's, but with even lower financial rewards for all but the top five players in any tournament.

'It's not a living, Jojo,' he shook his head. 'Most of the women who don't quit after a year or so on the tour have their own money, through marriage or family. No one breaks even through actual winnings, except for a very few. Take my advice: just relax and be calm. You'll find a job if you keep looking. You'll get married again—no man in his right mind would let you get away! You have a beautiful daughter to take care of—and you'll have more children. If you want to pursue a brilliant amateur career, I'm behind you all the way. But not the pro tour.'

Karen shook her head when she saw Joanna return home crestfallen.

'Carl's old-fashioned,' she laughed, wrinkling her freckled nose. 'He played the tour when big tournaments paid the winner five hundred dollars. He doesn't believe you'll rise to the top. I do.'

She insisted she would take care of Tina while Joanna competed in the L.P.G.A. Qualifying School. 'I've just finished a degree in English,' she joked. 'What does that qualify me for, if not babysitting? Go get 'em, Joanna!'

After two weeks of desperate training Joanna filled out her application, took the train to Greensboro with her clubs, and played the seventy-two hole tournament that was the Qualifying School. She placed second with a five-under-par two hundred and eighty-three and was given an amount of prize money which barely sufficed to pay her caddy.

But she had accomplished her purpose. On the basis of her second-place finish she was granted L.P.G.A. playing privileges—provided she paid her dues and insurance.

Taking a deep breath, she entered the Winston-Salem Classic the next week. She survived the cut after thirty-six holes, finished in a tie for tenth place, and returned to her Athens room with a check for two thousand three hundred dollars.

Joanna was on her way.

From every mistake she made, she learned. As the rounds and tournaments followed one another, the seasoned professionals she played with did their best to encourage her, and gradually the butterflies left her stomach.

She approached her profession with dedication, refining her strokes on the practice tee and putting green, training herself carefully and devising a high-energy diet which kept her slim and strong.

No longer the distracted schoolgirl who had played golf in a haze of fantasies, Joanna executed her shots with complete concentration now. She analysed her effort on each hole, comparing her performance to the result she had planned.

Her hard work paid off. Before long her tempo and mechanics had reached a point of subtle perfection which amazed those who saw her play. Experts compared her fluid swing to that of the legendary Joyce Wethered, and her fairway woods and long irons were declared to be the most uncannily accurate in the history of women's golf.

And her winnings reflected her skill and consistency. After two seasons on the tour she made a down-payment on the house outside Sarasota, whose proximity to so many courses in the warm Florida winter would facilitate her practice. Karen, overjoyed at having sold a novelette to a national magazine, came along 'for the ride'.

By her fourth year on the tour Joanna was an international star, visible to the public not only during competition but also through endorsements and in the press, where she was eagerly sought as an articulate spokesperson for women in golf and a penetrating analyst of the game itself.

Affiliated as touring professional with Nakoma Springs Golf Club, near her new home, Joanna was a respected member of the community, and gave her time to charitable causes whenever possible.

She was a happy young woman—but a realist. Her disastrous marriage had left her scarred and brittle. She was in no mood to let her yearnings to feel wanted lead her into calamity again. Deep inside she wondered whether she would ever be happy in love.

'Maybe I'm accident-prone where men are concerned,' she shrugged, tempted to stop believing that the man she might some day long to give herself to would want to have her.

But she had Tina. Nothing could take that away from her.

Her only worry was that the child had no father. Tina was growing more unique, more special every day. She was so tactful, so serious and sweet, never complaining about being a child of divorce, or about Joanna's long absences in the spring and summer ... Sometimes it seemed as though this wise little daughter was comforting her mother for having uncorrectable failings.

But Joanna pushed these thoughts to the back of her mind, reasoning that no one's life is perfect, and that a woman could not ask more of herself than to do her best for those she loved.

Chris had grown into a lovely young woman, married a hard-working local man in Crane and had two children on whom Ellen doted. Protesting that the money Joanna sent her was always too much, Ellen remained in her old apartment and continued to work at her old job. The family seemed happy.

As one year followed another Joanna's fame increased. Her lovely face and figure captivated millions of fans who saw behind them her struggles, her strength, and her courage—as well as her vulnerability.

For her mystique as the 'winner–loser' of women's golf was now a firmly established facet of her public image. Brilliant and even incomparable though her golf game might be, something kept her from winning.

Something.

She had become almost as expert at deflecting the

question of her failure to win as she was at striking a fairway shot or lining up a putt. But it would not go away, and she knew it.

Thus life went on until the day Reid Armstrong appeared.

CHAPTER FOUR

'WAKE up, Joanna—wake up, now! That's right . . .'

It was not like being awake, she decided as the recovery room nurse's hurried features smiled down at her. She struggled to answer, but moving her lips was like walking over a mountain of cotton balls.

Satisfied, the nurse disappeared.

Joanna drifted into oblivion, her eyes open like those of a wounded animal.

When next she woke she was in her room. Black night loomed beyond the window blinds. The T.V. hung on the wall like a haggard, prying eye.

Joanna rang for the nurse, and after many minutes an unfamiliar young woman entered and told her to rest. Dr Diehl would be in tomorrow morning.

Joanna's knee was heavily bandaged and elevated. She could no longer feel the intense pain behind the kneecap. But she could not feel anything else, either, except the dullness and apathy and confusion and nagging inner ache that seemed the essence of life in this hospital. The stab behind the kneecap had simply settled into the general throb of her battered body.

Am I cured? she dared to hope for an instant. But the effort was too much, and emotionally exhausted, she closed her eyes.

The elevated knee would not allow her to toss and turn. She lay immobile, straying half asleep from one sinister dream landscape to another, as the night's darkest hours passed her by.

The next morning Dr Diehl appeared at last—and

Joanna knew instantly what the forced smile on his thin lips meant.

'The news is good,' he said unconvincingly. 'You're going to be fine, Joanna. You'll need a lot of physical therapy, and you'll come out of this with some residual weakness in that knee, but you'll be able to live normally.'

He began discussing aspects of the surgery and her convalescence as the nurse busied herself behind him. Joanna could see he was in a hurry to leave her; the pleading looks she could not help sending in his direction did not seem to slow him down.

'What about . . . my golf?' she asked at last, feeling as though she were breaching a taboo subject.

He shook his head with a pained frown.

'Joanna,' he said argumentatively, 'you have multiple sprains, very serious ones, in your knee ligaments, both lateral and medial. I suspect some microscopic tears in your cartilage, and I know for sure that your patella tendon has been torn. Now, your knee is going to recover, but it's going to be on the weak side—weak enough to hurt your confidence in it, and that's going to hurt your golf game. You may still play, but not at a championship level. I hate to have to tell you this, but you may as well know it right now. I don't want you holding on to false hopes.'

He smiled patronisingly. 'Try and look on the bright side,' he urged. 'You've had a brilliant career in golf, but all athletic careers have to end some time. Now, you're a beautiful, desirable young woman; you're sure to get married again one of these days soon. You have a lovely young daughter. Life doesn't end without professional golf.'

If I were a man, Joanna mused bitterly, *he would sing a different tune*.

But anger availed little against the terror inside her.

I will play again, she thought desperately. *I must play again*.

No one had warned her about post-operative depression. She felt a curious letting-go in all her nerves, a desire to lie down and stop trying to cope with the brutal exhaustion of each new thought, each impression.

And now, with the whole world hammering nightmarishly at her last reserves of strength, she realised that she must greet Tina and say goodbye to her in a single moment. It was Joanna herself who had insisted that Karen take Tina back to Sarasota today. The child had already missed three days of school on her account, and the school year was at its end. Now that the surgery was over and pronounced successful, there was no reason for her to be here.

'Mommy, is your knee feeling better?' the little girl asked hesitantly after Karen had brought her in.

'Much better, honey,' said Joanna, forcing a happy smile. 'Be good to Karen, now. And you and Suzanne behave yourselves with Miss Ward. And don't forget to give her the flowers on your last day.'

'I won't,' Tina promised, still holding her mother's hand as she popped from the bedside to the floor.

Screwing up her courage, Joanna planted a brisk goodbye kiss on her daughter's cheek and patted her shoulder with a black-and-blue hand.

'And save your papers!' she called after her, stricken to think that she would not see Tina's last two weeks of third-grade work until long after it was done.

A moment later they were gone, Karen having affectionately steered her vibrant little charge through the door with a hand on each pigtail.

Apparently having decided not to leave Joanna time for morbid thoughts, Reid appeared almost instantly, his teasing grin lighting up the room as he placed a colourful flower arrangement by the window.

'Well, Joanna,' he announced blithely, 'looks like it's just you and me.'

Joanna burst into tears.

For what seemed a long time Reid sat on the edge of her bed, the gentle touch of his hand on her own doing little to assuage her grief.

'I can't say that's the most delighted reception I've ever had,' he joked when her tear-stained eyes finally turned to him.

'It wasn't you,' she sighed her disapproval of his humour. 'It's just ... just ...' Renewed sobs of consternation choked her.

'Take it easy, now,' he murmured, touching a finger to her cheek. 'Just relax. You're going to be fine.'

She shook her head in impotent dissent. 'The doctor,' she stammered. 'He says ...'

'I know what he says,' nodded Reid. 'And I'll tell you something, just between you and me. Bob Diehl is an expert at what he does—the best, in fact. But athletes are machines to him. He doesn't understand desire. I know, Joanna. He treated me for a lumbar disc problem when I was a sophomore in college. He told me I'd have to quit football altogether. But during the next two years I caught fifty passes and scored more points than anybody except the kicker.'

Joanna struggled to weigh his words coherently. Life seemed so utterly black that she had hardly the energy even to meet his gaze.

'Listen,' he went on. 'I've seen your chart, Joanna. You've got some sprains and some possible cartilage damage. I've known dozens of athletes who have played out their careers with similar problems.' He laughed. 'I'll bet you didn't know that among the entire outfield of the New York Yankees last year there wasn't a single intact knee cartilage.'

He grew more serious. 'And,' he said, 'to tell the

honest truth, Bob is a little old-fashioned where women are concerned. When he looks at a shapely leg like yours, he doesn't think of grinding out months on the pro golf tour. He thinks of a happy home and lots of children.'

There was softness behind his probing eyes as he smiled down at her.

'So you see,' he concluded, 'Bob doesn't see what you're made of under that pretty face of yours. I do. You'll come out of this good as new—if you want to.'

Joanna nodded exhaustedly.

'More than that,' he added, 'you're coming out of this *better* than new. I intend to see to it.' He grinned. 'You're a fine athlete, but you need someone to watch out for you. You've been going it alone for too long.'

Against her better judgment Joanna let her tired hand rest in his. She hated to hear him speak of her dependence. He was all health and handsome strength, while she felt beaten to a pulp, black and blue all over and perhaps damaged beyond repair. In his boundless confidence he seemed so foreign, so alien—yet he alone offered her the encouragement she so desperately needed.

Though her depression told her he should leave her to her dark despair and go about his sunny business, she wanted him to stay. Manipulative and arrogant he might be—but he was on her side. He believed in her.

But what if he's wrong?

She banished the awful thought and, with a sigh of uncertain gratitude, let her half-closed eyes linger on his tanned face.

Two days later Joanna was allowed to leave the hospital. She barely slept a wink the night before her departure, so great was her eagerness to get on with her unknowable future.

'Are you really sure about this arrangement?' she had asked Reid during visiting hours. 'I feel a little funny about coming to your house. I'm ... imposing,' she concluded, her liberated ideas not allowing her to give voice to her scruples.

'Not at all,' he shrugged. 'It's a business arrangement. That's what my house is for, more than anything. I'm a middle-man, Joanna; I bring people there all the time on business visits. Besides, Tina and Karen are coming soon. And,' he added with a wry smile, 'if you're worried about the proprieties, Mrs Hughes, my housekeeper, will be moving in for the duration of your stay. She'll chaperone us, if you feel you can't trust yourself.'

'Very funny!' Joanna reproved him, her lips pursed in irritation.

At eight a.m. he wheeled her through the hospital's sliding doors and into a hot North Carolina morning. The air was thick with humidity, but to Joanna it smelled fresh as spring after the hospital's antiseptic coldness.

At her insistence Reid left the air-conditioning off in the large sedan he had brought. Joanna's plush seat reclined deliciously, and the soft breeze coming through the vent caressed her legs and arms with lulling sweetness.

'We'll go straight down 95 to Beaufort County,' Reid decided. 'Not the most picturesque route in the world, but it's the fastest way. I imagine you've driven it a hundred times on your way to tournaments.'

With a glance to his right he smiled. Joanna was fast asleep.

She awoke at the shudder of the engine being turned off. Reid was leaning back in his seat, his smile glimmering beneath a quirked brow. She could smell the ocean.

'Where are we?' she asked, rubbing her eyes sleepily.

'Beaufort,' he said. 'You're a lady who knows how to sleep—you've been out the whole way.'

Joanna looked out the window to see a magnificent seascape framed by green hills that led gently down to beaches and marshland lush with long grass and elders. Beneath the stands of pines she could make out palmetto and magnolia trees. Were it not for the pastures in the hills the scene would have looked totally wild. It was a fantastic display of natural beauty, uniting all the elements that made this part of the country famous.

'Why have we stopped here?' she asked. 'It's beautiful.'

'Glad you think so,' nodded Reid. 'The big pine forest down the beach gave it its name. This is it, Joanna: Black Woods.'

Joanna stared at the landscape, trying to imagine it as the setting for a championship golf layout. Gulls and terns wheeled in the air over the gently washing surf. In the distance a heron stood alone, desultorily preening its feathers. She saw a sandpiper on the rocky beach. The ocean breeze was heavy, balmy. It would blow a driven golf ball steadily inland, off course.

The marshes were the habitat of many of these birds and animals. Who would imagine what effect bulldozers and artificial water systems might have on their lives? Would some of the sea-birds be driven away to quieter waters if changes in the shore foliage affected the fish swimming here?

Seeing two creeks snake their way down the hills towards the ocean, Joanna recalled Reid's description of the layout as being rich in natural water hazards.

'Quite a showplace, isn't it?' he asked.

'Yes,' she said, fascinated by the delicately ordered ecology that made the place unique.

'Worried about keeping it that way?' he asked, guessing her thoughts.

Sleepy and irritable, she glanced at him. 'Someone should be,' she said.

'Good,' he smiled. 'Perhaps you'd better think about taking on this job. Otherwise I may have to settle for an architect who will mutilate the whole landscape just to get a course out of it.'

'Don't make it my responsibility,' Joanna protested. 'I haven't agreed to anything yet.'

'As a professional,' he said, 'you must have played some awful layouts along with the good ones, so I'm sure you'd want to see that a site like this was served well.'

'How do I know women will even be allowed to play this course?' asked Joanna on a querulous impulse. 'How do I know the country club they put here would even accept me as a member? It may interest you to know, if you didn't already, that ninety per cent of the clubs in this country will not accept single women members.'

Reid raised an eyebrow. 'That's news to me,' he said. 'But, come to think of it, the golf world is pretty old-fashioned, isn't it?'

'That's the understatement of the year,' sighed Joanna. 'There are only a handful of women club pros in the country, and they have to live with constant harassment. Most of the championship courses are designed only with men in mind. The women's tees are ill-kept and sloppily placed, so that our skills aren't fairly tested at all when we play. And I can think of some country clubs where men play big tournaments, and women are not allowed to play at all.'

His nod of assent was touched by teasing humour, as though he were more amused than anything else by her resentment.

'I don't see what's so funny about it,' she said crossly. 'Women have had an uphill battle in golf, and still do. I don't mind telling you I wonder whether your investors will seriously consider any design done by a woman.' She folded her arms in frustration.

There was sympathy in his laughing eyes.

'That knee has you pretty worried, doesn't it?' he asked, his penetration shocking her.

'Who said I was worried?' she fumed, irked to see her thoughts divined so easily by a virtual stranger. 'Perhaps I was. Perhaps I am.'

'Life is full of obstacles, Joanna,' he said through his smile. 'Unfair ones, to boot, and for both sexes. Sometimes there's nothing to be done about them. But it is important that you learn not to be your own worst enemy.'

'What's that supposed to mean?' she asked, angered to hear him trivialise her complaints.

'Maybe this golf club will be as stodgy as any other,' he said. 'But you can make sure the course is well designed. You have that power. And when and if you play it as a competitor, you have the power to win. Nobody can beat you—except yourself.'

His look was suddenly intense. Unable to make him out, Joanna glanced uncertainly into his dark irises.

'But you're not going to win anything,' he smiled, 'until we get you a cup of hot tea and some aspirin, and something to eat. Shall we go home?'

As he threw the car into gear she reflected that once again he had hit the nail on the head. Underneath her vexation was a wave of pain which had gained in intensity during her long sleep.

Home, as it turned out, was an extraordinarily beautiful two-storey house whose white clapboard was broken by large picture windows. From inside Joanna realised what their purpose was. Since the house stood on a hill overlooking Saint Helena Sound, superb views of sky and ocean were framed by those windows—views cleverly taken up by glass breakfronts and bookcases inside the house's brightly lit rooms.

Some of the paintings on the walls even had glass frames intentionally arranged to superimpose reflected seascapes over the pictures underneath. The result was that the whole place had an oceanic look, inside and out.

Hobbled by her unfamiliar crutches, Joanna went into the spacious kitchen and was greeted by Mrs Hughes, the housekeeper who doubled as live-in cook when Reid had guests. Her soft Southern drawl ringing with particular charm against the image of her greying hair and bright eyes, she extended a hand.

'I'm delighted to meet you,' she said. 'You won't remember, Miss Lake, but my daughter Katie sent you a fan letter once, and you wrote her the nicest response. She absolutely idolises you. I may have been presumptuous, but since we live right down the road I told her she might be able to meet you, and your daughter when she arrives. Katie would be happy to show her around these parts.'

Helping her down the stairs with a strong arm around her waist, Reid showed Joanna the basement. On the padded floor were benches and weights, Nautilus and Cybex machines for leg lifts and presses, and a padded table for other exercises.

'We're all ready for you,' he said, 'thanks to Virginia. In a week or so we'll get to work on your hamstrings and quadriceps, and of course both knees.' He smiled complacently. 'Yes, you're going to have a lot of fun here, Joanna. Bicycling, walking, swimming, jogging on the beach . . . Why, I'll have you running up and down those stairs in no time!'

'Makes me tired just to think of it,' she sighed. But her athlete's eye told her the elaborate machinery he had assembled aimed at more than mere physical therapy in the wake of an accident. In this room was all the wherewithal to train her for competition.

'This place,' she said when they were upstairs once more. 'It's lovely, but, if you don't mind my saying so, it doesn't seem . . .'

'Lived-in?' Reid laughed. 'I'm afraid you're right. I bought it three years ago because I thought it would be a good investment. I came here on business, saw this place at a bargain price, and bought it on an impulse. Then those ocean views began to get to me, so I stayed here and kept my apartment in Atlanta as well. I never got around to selling the house. So I'm of two minds—I can't get rid of it, and I can't make a home out of it.' He smiled. 'Just having you here brightens it up. When Tina gets here it will really seem human.'

He saw the reaction in her tired eyes.

'Missing her?' he asked.

Joanna nodded.

'Well,' he said, 'I'm sure Miss Ward is taking good care of her. And Abbas and Allie and Lynn and Suzanne will keep her company until the end of school.'

'How did you know all that?' asked Joanna, amazed to hear him reel off the names of Tina's friends so blandly.

'Tina told me herself,' he laughed, 'while you were in your Demerol trance at the hospital. Friends and school seemed the logical thing to ask a little girl about on the first meeting. Especially a girl who might be scared about her mom and be able to use some distraction. Why, I know all about Miss Ward. I know she used to be a stewardess, and she took a trip to Hawaii last summer and got caught in a hurricane, and she can be rough about math but is nice about reading. I even know about the Embarrass-Kings.'

Joanna smiled to hear the girls' name for the intimidating fourth and fifth graders on his lips. Obviously he had been good for Tina during long hours that must have been quite frightening to her. Perhaps his promises about horseback riding and swimming had not been so irresponsible after all.

'Tina says she's very beautiful,' he was saying.

'Who?'

'Miss Ward.'

'Oh,' said Joanna. 'Yes, she's very attractive, for your information. If you're interested,' she added wryly, 'I'm sure Tina would be happy to introduce you if you're ever in our area.'

Reid made a hands-off gesture. 'I have more than enough women in my life, thank you,' he said. 'What with you here, and Tina on her way as soon as school is out . . .'

'I'll just bet you keep busy,' Joanna laughed. 'I hope we won't be in the way.' Indeed, she thought, the curiously impersonal furnishings of the house, beautiful as they were, seemed to suggest the lifestyle of a handsome, busy bachelor who enjoyed seeing many women while committing himself to none.

'Come on,' he said, seeing the fatigue in her eyes. 'I'll show you your bedroom. After you've had a nice nap you can call home to tell them you got here safe. Then we'll think about dinner.'

Joanna hardly saw the beautiful bedroom whose pastel curtains were closed against the waning sunlight. She sank gratefully on to the large bed as Reid placed a quilted comforter over her, his large hand touching her bandaged knee with delicate concern.

She looked up at him from her helpless position on the spread. Pain and exhaustion had conspired to put her in a susceptible mood. How handsomely erect he was in his dauntless confidence as he stood over her in the shadows of this foreign place! Here in his own home, he was prepared to repair her damaged body at all costs, to palpate it and work it with his knowing hands until it was strong enough to suit him, no matter what her doctor thought about her condition . . .

Since the moment he had entered her life, it seemed, the world she knew had flown from her, replaced all at once by strange new vistas at whose centre he loomed, tall and powerful and maddeningly indispensable.

He closed the door behind him, his smile shining down upon her for a last second. Then he disappeared into the unseen corridors of this odd, anonymous house which was to be the site of her doubts and sufferings, her hoped-for rehabilitation, the sleepless nights of her worry about the future—and perhaps unforeseen temptations.

'If only Tina were here,' she thought as dreams overtook her.

CHAPTER FIVE

'LIFT. Good . . . again. Does that hurt?'

' . . .'

'All right, wait a minute. Good. Lift again. Does that hurt?'

The infuriating voice of command was deep and relaxed. Joanna shook her head, too breathless to articulate an answer.

The pain in her thigh was unbearable, yet she knew that somehow she had enough strength left for the last two repetitions. Reid never chose too much weight; just enough to make life an agony.

'Good. Two more.' A dry finger touched the sweaty flesh of her leg, testing the sinews above the left knee.

'Does that hurt?' the maddening voice asked for what seemed the thousandth time.

'*Yes!*' she gasped, beside herself with frustration as she lifted her leg against the padded bar for the last time. Her back arched and straining, she was held into the machine by the safety belt about her waist. Reid seemed as much a part of this crazy bondage as the machine itself. 'What do you take me for?' she asked angrily, her halting breaths coming in little jerks. 'Some kind of masochist?'

'No,' he smiled without taking his eyes from her knee. 'Just a feminist.'

'Very funny,' she sighed, feeling drops of perspiration flow down her exhausted back and along the thigh whose quadriceps muscle was in a constant state of trauma from the exercises he made her do.

Upstairs Tina was probably chatting with Virginia or

reading one of the favourite books she had brought. Later she would go riding or swimming with Reid while Joanna rested and exercised on her own.

It had been three weeks since the day Joanna had come here from the hospital, and nearly six days since the long-awaited morning of Tina's arrival. Already a new routine had set in, admittedly necessary but far from what Joanna would have desired.

She saw Tina in the morning and at noon, unless an outing with Reid or Katie Hughes kept her away for lunch. At dinnertime the child would bring her tired mother up to date on her day's activities, eating savoury dishes cooked by Virginia while Joanna made do with bland low-calorie meals.

In the evenings Joanna relaxed in an orthopaedic easy chair and looked on as Tina sat in Reid's lap, read him passages from her books, or watched the classic movies offered by his television subscription service.

Whenever Joanna saw Tina, it seemed, she saw new evidence of her easy closeness with Reid. His deep voice and ready humour clearly delighted the little girl no less than the powerful arms that swept her up for hugs or piggyback rides, or merely to hold her out for admiration by his dark eyes. She held his hand happily when they walked together, her energetic little frame dwarfed by his long limbs.

'She takes after you,' he confided to Joanna. 'She's very precise and methodical about her books and her dolls. But there's a strong creative imagination underneath all those brains.' He darted his teasing glance to her reflective features. 'Of course,' he added, 'she's a lot more trusting than you.'

'She's had less experience,' Joanna returned.

'I guess you could say that,' Reid allowed. 'But sometimes I wonder whether it wouldn't be better to be surprised by trouble than to expect it all the time.'

'Oh, I don't know,' said Joanna. 'I've had more than my share of surprises lately.'

'I suppose you have,' he nodded, his inscrutable smile caressing the face and slender body which still bore black-and-blue areas under a sallow complexion.

After three relaxed days spent bringing Joanna up on all her news and ogling the furnishings in Reid's rooms, Karen had left for Sarasota. She intended to oversee the house and whatever business came up—including the buying of a new car—and at the same time to finish the mystery novel she had been working on for many months. Joanna felt a pang of guilt at the life that kept Karen from her own work, and was glad to see her leave for a few weeks of welcome solitude.

Her crutches gone now, Joanna limped around the house in futile search of amusements to pass the time when she was not working out or resting. Having set up a handsome design table in the study, complete with fluorescent lamp, blueprint paper, and maps of the Black Woods layout's elevations, drainage and soil content, Reid made a point of not offering her any interesting books or magazines to read, so that her curiosity would be drawn ever closer to the prospective design.

He drove her to the layout, showed her how to take his jeep there when he was not available, and discussed golf course architecture with her, his studied casualness belying his obvious hope that she would get to work in earnest before long.

But in her private thoughts about the beautiful landscape she had hit a snag. As a player she had complained for years about the unfair placement of women's tees on championship golf courses. Now she realised it would be virtually impossible to design a single hole whose dimensions would not be unfair either to the longer-hitting male player or the weaker female.

One sex or the other must suffer, it seemed, unless separate courses were designed for each. No wonder, she mused bitterly, that country clubs exclusively for women had sprung up over the years to match those reserved for men.

Her intellectual quandary became truly paralysing when added to her acute awareness that she had absolutely no experience as an architect. She could not imagine herself giving the order that would transform the Black Woods' virgin perfection into something man-made and perhaps environmentally disastrous.

So she hesitated, distracted from her scruples by lingering pain and the exhaustion brought on by her spartan training regimen. The monotony of her days, combined with traces of post-operative depression which overtook her when she contemplated her damaged body in the bedroom mirror, sapped her energy.

It was one thing to jealously covet the cheeseburgers and pizzas Tina enjoyed so blithely with Reid, while Joanna suffered with her lean broiled meats and cottage cheese. It was quite another to recall that underneath these temporary deprivations lurked the very real possibility that her career was over for ever.

She had visited Dr Diehl in Charleston often enough to know that he considered her future in golf a lost cause. The pressure of secretly hoping for a result of which her own physician had long since despaired threatened to reduce her to listless melancholy.

That was where Reid came in. Acutely aware of the obstacles Joanna faced, he knew how to keep her on edge mentally and physically, even if it meant needling her to ever greater progress through irritating manipulations. Now cajoling, now humiliating, now psychoanalysing her until she flushed with anger, he forced her to press forward with a programme whose ultimate goal was their unspoken secret.

Frustrated, Joanna remarked on the pain her exercises were producing in her uninjured leg.

'That's natural,' he told her. 'We can't neglect the good leg, or it will weaken. Besides, when we build the reflexes and muscle tone in the uninjured knee, the damaged one benefits from that biological information. It's called cross-education.'

'Can it work both ways?' asked Joanna dryly. 'Because my right leg is beginning to feel as though it's had an accident, too!'

She grew to hate the number twelve, because it was the invariable number of repetitions Reid required for each progressive-resistance exercise. As her strength increased he simply added more weight to the pulley system behind her back, making her feel all the weaker.

'You would have made a great coach,' she gasped one day after her twelfth knee lift. 'Your players would have murdered you in your sleep!'

'That's why I have you,' he drawled. 'You're too careful to commit murder. On the other hand, a little of the killer instinct is in every champion. Maybe we're moving you in the right direction.'

Joanna's back ached constantly from her workouts. Her thighs and calves were tight with pain when she walked up or down the basement stairs, jogging and bicycling were distressing ordeals in her condition. But her battered limbs were growing stronger, and she knew it. Their very discomfort was a positive sign. And as her body repaired itself she felt strange new longings in her woman's senses, flowerings of unforeseen awareness which disconcerted her—for they grew in intensity with each passing day.

'One more, now. Press. Is that hurting?'

With a final lunge, her back and legs in agony, her bandaged forearm pushing down on the seat beneath her, Joanna extended her knees for the twelfth and last time. The suspended weights clanged behind her back as she let the pedals fly towards her once more.

'Ouch!' she cried as a sharp stab of pain shot above her knee.

'Did you hurt yourself?' asked Reid, reaching a large hand to touch her throbbing thigh.

Too exhausted to answer, she shook her head. A lock of her blonde hair had escaped the sweatband over her forehead, and managed to fall across her cheek in her exertions. She pushed it away as his fingers ran delicately around her knee.

'Where does it hurt?' he asked coolly, his hands moving to compare the taped knee and its uninjured partner.

'Never mind,' she started to say. 'It was just . . .'

A gasp shook her before she could finish. As his dry fingers slipped over the soft skin behind the knees, a daunting surge of feeling had flashed through her, making speech impossible as it left her breathless with involuntary excitement.

'Are you sure?' he asked, palpating her more carefully now, his hands in search of swellings or suspicious areas of weakness. Hoping against hope that he was blind to the tumultuous response of female sinews under his unwitting caress, Joanna cursed the audible sign that had nearly given away what she had spent days and weeks trying to hide.

'Yes,' she said, catching her breath, 'I'm sure. If you'd just let me get out of this thing,' she added briskly, 'I'll be fine.'

Reid reached to undo the seatbelt around her waist as she sat panting before him, and his appraising eyes watched her knees work as she slipped out of the machine.

'Wait,' he placed a hand on her shoulder before she

could move towards the stairs. 'Sit a second while I look at you.'

Placing his hands under her arms, he lifted her on to the large padded table. Her flesh tingled to feel itself held by him, if only for a charged instant.

'Good,' he said, flexing and extending her knee slowly as she watched. 'No extra fluid. You're in better shape than I thought.' His fingers grazed the damp skin under her thigh, sending unseen thrills of pleasure up her spine, and she had to suppress the sigh that was on her lips. Her gaze lingered on the tanned skin of his face, the flecked blackness of his eyes under careless waves of tawny hair. The T-shirt he wore clung to powerful chest muscles and broad shoulders. He carried his athlete's body with graceful negligence, his movements lithe and easy.

From the first hours she had spent in this house Joanna had told herself he was not her type, and could not possibly attract her. But the passing days had brought unbidden revelations about her own instincts as well as the unsuspected depth of his virile charms.

Before long she had been forced to admit the truth to herself. She had been too long alone, too long without a man. The wildfires in her senses when Reid was near were too dizzying to deny.

Whether it was his odd amalgam of hard male attractiveness, puckish humour and demanding discipline that fascinated her, or merely an upsurge of sensual awareness due to her weakened condition, the result was the same: she was anything but indifferent to him.

And what was worse, the agony of wondering whether he suspected the guilty delight his touch kindled in her only seemed to make it the more insidiously captivating. As he watched her workouts with calm, evaluative eyes, his complacent supervision maddening her, she suffered the more to feel her treacherous body arch shamelessly before him, its exertions veering constantly towards more sinister rhythm.

Even her gasps of pain and exhaustion, as she sat strapped in the seat only inches from his probing eyes and hard man's limbs, were embarrassingly indistinguishable from the sounds of love.

She cursed the impudent caprice that leapt from inside her aching flesh to reveal itself, seeking to tempt him while bypassing her better judgment. Yet, try as she might, she could not quiet it.

'You're all right,' said Reid now, placing his hands around her waist to help her down from the table. In her eyes there must have been a trace of her bewilderment, for he met their sidelong gaze with a smile as he patted her hips in approval. And for a terrible, wonderful instant Joanna wondered whether the ferment inside her had somehow touched him after all. How odd it would be to see that handsome face draw close to her own, here in this cool underground room, under these harsh, strange lights which had come to signify their physical time together and the secret they shared. How indescribable to feel those dry, sensual lips touch her own, graze her cheek, her neck, and gently close her eyes . . .

'*Boo!*' The small, sharp voice sent a shock wave down her spine.

'Who's there?' Reid made a pretence of jumping back in fear.

Tina popped out from under the table and stood, hands on hips, in the centre of the room.

'What are you doing down here?' asked Joanna, suppressing her gasp of surprise.

'You're late,' said Tina through her mischievous smile. 'It's time for lunch.'

Reid was standing with his arms folded, as though at a safe distance. 'I thought you were a spook,' he said seriously.

'She can be when she wants to,' Joanna laughed.

'Well, that's fine,' he said. 'I told Mrs Hughes this house didn't have any spooks, and that I was thinking of getting rid of it in favour of more spooky accommodations. Now I can rest easy.'

A moment later they were ascending the narrow stairs, Reid coming last as Tina rushed ahead. Doubly embarrassed at having run the risk of being discovered in her disarray by her daughter as well as the man whose potent charms were playing such cruel tricks on her emotions, Joanna listened to the halting rhythm of her own breaths. Others must surely attribute it to the residual stress of her workout, she decided hopefully.

She alone must live with the knowledge of its true cause.

That night she helped Virginia prepare dinner and watched an old Bette Davis movie on television with Tina until fatigue overtook them both.

'I'm going out,' Reid told her after she had kissed Tina goodnight. 'I have an appointment to keep.' He looked at his Rolex watch, and back at Joanna sternly. 'It's about time for you to be in bed,' he said.

'Yes, Master,' she yawned. 'It will be a pleasure.'

Despite herself she wondered if he was keeping a date with one of the many women he must know. His attire, casual and roguishly handsome as always, gave no hint of his destination. It was possible, she knew, that he conducted serious business during his nocturnal outings so as to be free to spend time with her and Tina in the daytime. But he revealed nothing of his own doings.

As she started down the corridor to her room she could hear the surf washing quietly in the distance. Its balmy fragrance suffused the house, joining soft echoes to the delicious fatigue in her limbs.

She passed the study, with its maps and design tools shrouded in darkness. On an impulse she entered the room and turned on the fluorescent lamp craned over the table.

'Silly,' she thought, grasping a fine pencil with languorous fingers and pushing open the large sketch pad. 'Just a . . .'

Just a thought, she wanted to say to herself. But she had pulled back the chair and sat down, her hair flowing over her terrycloth robe, without realising what she was doing.

Her engineer's education came back to her as the sketch of a golf hole took shape under her pencil. Many was the time in college when she had agonised for hours over a problem in mathematics or physics, only to see it solve itself with striking ease when a single preconception was stripped away.

But she did not wait for thought to catch up with the force gathering inside her. Already the hole was nearly complete, with its bunkers and rough, the men's tee on the right, high up in the woods, the women's tee a hundred yards distant, behind the creek . . .

She pushed the design aside and began another. When that was finished she began another.

Briefly she reflected that the light was still on beside her bed, and that she should turn it out. She realised she was thirsty, and then forgot to get a glass of water. She did not hear Virginia go to bed.

The designs she was creating made sense, and yet they were not golf holes as anyone else understood them to be. But she did not wait to ponder their practicality. She continued drawing, afraid that this odd train of thought would pop out of her mind as quickly as it had popped in unless she followed it now.

She knew Reid would be angry with her if he found out she had stayed up so late. She resolved to turn out the light at the sound of his car—and then forgot her resolution.

The digital clock beside her showed three forty-five a.m. when a hand touched her shoulder, sending a shock through the naked limbs under her robe.

'You're up late.' Reid's voice was a pleasant murmur in her ear. She felt his long arms extend to the desk top before her as the warmth of his deep chest grazed her billowed hair.

In silence she watched him turn the pages of the sketch pad. Five golf holes, complete with estimated yardage, hazards, tees for men and women, and notated wind direction, passed before her eyes. His tanned fingers held the pages furled under the bright light as he studied the designs.

'Explain something to me,' he said, pointing to the first sketch. 'Isn't the women's tee even farther from the green than the men's? That seems strange.'

'Not at all,' Joanna replied, pointing to the page. 'You see, from the woman's angle the hole is a three hundred and forty-five-yard par four. Her tee shot is against the wind, so she has to lay up short of the water hazard, and then she has a difficult short iron to the green.'

'But the man's tee is so much closer,' Reid pointed out. 'Can't he reach the green in one?'

'Of course he can,' said Joanna. 'That's why, for him, the hole is par three.'

'You're kidding,' he shook his head. 'Different pars . . .'

'They're equalised later on,' Joanna explained. 'But the point is that the challenge is entirely different for each sex on each hole.'

For a long moment he turned the pages in silence.

'The male and female players,' he said at length, 'will hardly see each other, except on the greens.'

'Isn't that the case on a conventional course?' she asked, looking up at him. 'On this layout, at least, the challenge will be fair for both.'

In silence he evaluated her words.

'What do you think?' she asked at last.

'I think,' he smiled, raising her gently to her feet and brushing a strand of hair from her cheek, 'that you're a tired lady who needs some sleep.'

Joanna frowned at his noncommittal words.

'I also think you're a genius,' he went on, his dark eyes glittering in the shadows. 'I told you the Black Woods would make history with you as architect, and one of these days I'm going to congratulate myself for being so right.' His large hands rested warmly on her tired shoulders. 'And,' he added, drawing her to him, 'I think you're even prettier in person that you are on television.'

His embrace was easy and amiable, welcome as his confidence in her. But the Black Woods had flown from her consciousness, their expanse as limitless as her wonderings about where he had been tonight, and with whom.

Only the mad tremors under her skin remained, along with her fear that he might feel them, and her forlorn certainty that it was only as a friend that Reid held her thus.

CHAPTER SIX

'LET's go, little one,' Reid's deep voice echoed down the hallway.

'Coming,' came Tina's murmur as she put down her book and skipped out of her room.

Reid stood with Virginia in the kitchen, putting the finishing touches to a large wicker picnic basket and beach bag. Both were dressed lightly, for the July morning outside was so hot that only the ocean breeze made normal activity bearable.

'Sure you'll be all right here alone?' Reid asked Joanna. 'You can come along, you know. A day at the beach won't hurt you. As a matter of fact, you look too pale. You're spending too much of your time in the basement.'

'Then you'd better put a sun lamp down there,' Joanna joked, 'because you know you'll never let me out long enough to get any sun.' She shook her head. 'No, you all go on. I'll keep the home fires burning while I do my own work.'

Reid stooped to check the tape on her knee. He had wrapped it with extra care this morning, as he knew she would be doing her exercises alone.

'If anything comes up,' he said, 'give my answering service a call. They may know where we end up. Otherwise, tell anyone who calls that I'm gone for the day.'

Thirteen-year-old Katie appeared at the door, her freckled face aglow with her pleasure over the day's outing.

'I guess we're all here,' said Reid, his eyes resting on Tina as she hugged her mother.

'Have a good time,' said Joanna, kissing the little girl's cheek. 'And don't swim out too far. Stay with Mr Armstrong or Katie.'

A moment later they had all left, bound for a long day in the sun on Hilton Head Island. After watching the car crawl down the hill Joanna turned back to the kitchen.

Downstairs the machines waited, along with the weighted boot Joanna used for her quadriceps and knee exercises. In the refrigerator were the lean meat and hardboiled eggs reserved for her solitary lunch.

In the study down the hall waited the Black Woods design. All eighteen holes were in place now, each one like an embryo whose final features are not yet evident, but whose destiny is planned in advance. Only a few short weeks had passed since her nocturnal breakthrough, and yet Joanna had seen the entire layout come to life in her imagination with miraculous rapidity.

The experience was as fearsome as it was fulfilling. Almost overnight, it seemed, she had found herself attempting something of which she had never dreamed herself capable. And now the process was growing inside her and on the pages she sketched, real and beautiful and unspeakably exhausting.

All that was required for the Black Woods to come into being as an inspired, aesthetically revolutionary test of golf was that its architect remain at a fever pitch of mental energy until its birth pangs were over.

The task seemed impossibly big for one inexperienced woman. Yet it was being accomplished, one day at a time, under Joanna's pencil. Somehow she knew she would hang on until the last idea, the final touch, had come to her.

But today she was not going to work on the Black Woods design. Nor was she going to touch the exercise machines downstairs.

Joanna had another plan. And now that the others were gone, certain to be miles away all day long, she intended to put it into action.

She prowled the house one last time before leaving. Though she expected to be back by early afternoon, she felt a furtive impulse to make sure everything was in order.

A friendly letter from Carl Jaeger lay on the desk beside the design table. On an odd whim Joanna had decided not to tell Carl that she had agreed to undertake the design. Though he had long supported her in whatever she chose to do professionally, she somehow could not bring herself to tell him she had taken on so ambitious a project. In the wake of her immediate physical problems, her sally into architecture seemed premature.

Indeed, she thought as she passed the kitchen bulletin board, to the golf world at large her playing days appeared over. Reid had pinned up a morosely triumphant article by Ron Lieber announcing Joanna's imminent retirement, based on supposed confidential information from sources at Holy Family Hospital.

'I'll be the one to announce my retirement, Ron,' Joanna had told him angrily when she called to protest his report, 'not an unnamed source who sat in on my surgery.'

'Suit yourself,' he had shrugged. 'I have newspapers to sell, Miss Lake.'

Alongside the article Reid had affixed a wire service photo of Joanna jogging on the beach. It had been published in sports sections under the headline, *Can She Come Back?*

Reid found the media's efforts to make hay out of Joanna's plight amusing. 'Wait until you actually return to competition,' he laughed. 'The publicity will be

unbelievable. They have you dead and buried now, the
better to resurrect you when you show them you can
play. It's all dollars and cents to them,' he added with
his cheerful cynicism, 'and it will probably net you some
new endorsements when you're back.'

Also on the cork board was a colour snapshot of
Joanna with Reid and Tina on a Beaufort street. It had
been taken during their first week together, when
Joanna still bore all the overt marks of her accident.

She smiled now to recall her embarrassment at being
seen in public in her bruised and bandaged condition.
Since she was in the company of a man and a child, she
feared she gave the impression of a battered wife whose
scars bespoke raging quarrels with her spouse. Indeed,
when a strange man approached, his features clouded
by concern, she wondered in alarm whether he wanted
to offer her his protection.

'I beg your pardon,' he asked, 'but aren't you Joanna
Lake?'

Suppressing a laugh at her own silly imaginings,
Joanna nodded. The man, a tourist staying on Hilton
Head with his family, asked to be permitted to take a
picture of her for his daughters, who would be
heartbroken to have missed her. Apparently impressed
by the threesome she made with Reid and Tina, he
insisted on snapping them together. Two weeks later the
snapshot came in the mail along with a letter of thanks.

Joanna contemplated it now, a trifle disconcerted by
its penetrating revelation of the pattern that had
emerged in the weeks after it was taken. Tina stood
comfortably between the two adults, her hand nestling
in Reid's large palm with candid trust and confidence.
With her sandy hair and dark eyes she could easily pass
for his daughter, and Joanna for his wife. Indeed, under
the softening influence of Tina's warm feelings for him,
Joanna herself seemed to smile a sidelong glance of

reluctant affection his way, even as her eyes looked directly into the camera.

And in her gold-flecked irises there was a curious, palpable mixture of discomfort in the wake of her operation, dread over her uncertain future, and visible, elfin expectancy, as though she knew a secret she was hiding even from herself.

She turned away, unnerved by the photo's prescient capturing of so many intimate feelings. From her first meeting with Reid she had decided that he was an alien creature, a self-interested wheeler-dealer worlds apart from what she admired in a man. Yet a wilful little part of her, charmed by his humour, his understanding, and his closeness with Tina, reached out persistently to him.

'He's not my type,' she told herself, frightened by sensual stirrings which seemed to beckon her to perverse and merely physical enjoyment of his handsome body. But even that scruple, she realised, was insufficient, for her dangerous impulses went beyond the aching need his nearness created in her woman's flesh. It was as though that prohibited little corner of her had made up its mind that he was, after all, her type—that she felt and wanted to feel married to him, there on the public street where all could see, and that, were it not for the absence of one delicious pleasure that all husbands and wives enjoy together, they would indeed have made the perfect family with the little girl who stood so naturally and gracefully between them . . .

Confused, she thought how odd it was that Tina, whose obvious attachment to Reid was magnetising her own relationship with him, simultaneously acted along with Virginia as chaperone in this beautiful, quiet house where temptation might at last have overwhelmed Joanna's resistance had she been alone with Reid.

And even that daunting notion was mere wishful thinking, she decided with a shrug. Reid's very blitheness in his dealings with her made clear that her femininity was the least of his concerns. When he complimented her on her good looks he did so with deliberate indifference, as though he were assessing her professional attributes. It was as a businessman that he calculated her talents and sought to prick her ambition.

He wanted his course design, she realised. His sense of responsibility about her accident decreed that he see to her convalescence. For the moment he was pleased to enjoy the female companionship she afforded him, and to give free rein to his natural affinity with Tina.

But it went no further. The very elegance of this house, so cool and impersonal, was clear evidence that Reid kept his private self far removed from the guests he received there.

In confidence Virginia had told her a story related by a business acquaintance who had stayed for a weekend during her first year with Reid.

'He told me Reid came from a wealthy old family,' she said, 'but broke with his parents in a pretty scandalous way. They had him engaged to a girl from an even richer family. Why he went along with it as long as he did, no one knew—though the girl was apparently mad about him. He broke the engagement all at once, practically leaving her at the altar. When his father threatened to disinherit him—an idle threat made in anger, so the story goes—Reid jumped at the chance, as though it was an offer he couldn't refuse. He finished school on his football scholarship, went into business— strictly as a middle-man, without ever working for anybody or owning a firm himself—and became a great success.

'I've been his housekeeper three years now, and I don't claim to understand him,' Virginia admitted, 'but I get the feeling he can't bear to be manipulated by others. So he goes his own way and does the manipulating himself. He's very careful, and very private.'

Virginia did not amplify on the social life of which she must surely know something, but Joanna took for granted that Reid's many conquests with the opposite sex had taken him no nearer to marriage. Clearly he preferred his unhampered bachelorhood to a husband's entangling obligations.

With a sigh she darted a last glance at the writing desk beneath the bulletin board. A letter from her insurance company lay where she had left it yesterday, accompanied by a settlement cheque many hundreds of dollars below the price of her new station wagon, which was still in Sarasota with Karen. Joanna had insisted on a model with heavy duty suspension and a powerful engine regardless of the expense, for she liked a responsive vehicle and a safe one.

Tina had named the new car Michael, sight unseen. Her choice of a masculine name in the wake of Louisa's violent end was not lost on her mother.

Most of all Joanna was acutely aware that she would earn nothing as a player this summer. Endorsement offers would be hard to come by if she did not return to the tour soon. Her affiliation with Nakoma Springs must eventually dissolve unless her competitive career was restored. Indeed, years of hardship like those she had known as a girl might lie in wait for her and Tina unless she found a way to prove Robert Diehl's dour prognosis wrong.

That was why she could wait no longer to test the strength of her knee. Reid's painfully disciplined training programme had done its work, and Joanna could lift her weighted boot or push at a Nautilus bar with alacrity. But she had no way of knowing whether the tendons and ligaments could stand the strain of a good, hard golf swing and brisk follow-through, repeated over and over again as competitive play required.

Today she would know the answer.

She did not like to imagine Reid's wrath if he found out what she intended. *He won't find out*, she decided with a grim glance into the study. Reid assumed she would be working on the design today. If he returned to find the jeep gone, he would think she had taken it to the Black Woods.

But she would be home long before he returned.

She drove along the coast road to the spot she had passed several times before. She knew what she was looking for.

It was a golf centre, including a driving range, miniature golf course for tourists and their children, and par three layout. She had never bothered to notice its name.

She parked the jeep in the gravel lot and walked through the enormous morning heat past the Coke machines beside which young boys stood munching potato chips out of bags they had bought inside. The driving range was nearly empty. In the distance the ball collector drove slowly back and forth, picking up the red-striped practice balls as its driver sat behind his heavy mesh screen.

The range proprietor looked at Joanna without expression as he took her money and handed over an ancient, battered women's driver and a bucket of balls. The heat seemed to have ruined his business for the day. He stared forlornly over his tattooed arms at the television in the corner, knowing he would sell no more than a few miniature golf rounds and bags of potato chips or popcorn until twilight. Only young boys were out in this fainting heat.

Joanna walked quickly to a cubicle, poured the painted balls into the dispenser, and used the club head to pull down the chute which deposited the first ball on the rubber tee.

She stood at address, rocking back and forth to test her balance, aware of the tightness of her left knee, and perhaps of a fugitive weakness she had never felt there before.

Never mind, she told herself, pursing her lips in concentration. *Just hit it*.

Before she could begin her backswing a sight beyond the concession stand made her shrink with furtive suddenness behind the cubicle's screened partition. On the first hole of the miniature golf course a tall man was standing with a little girl. Bending over her slender body, he was showing her how to hold a putter.

For a panicky second Joanna had thought that, incredibly, they were Reid and Tina, and she smiled ruefully at her error. But all at once it occurred to her that she might be recognised here. Her ponytail and taped knee would give away her identity to anyone familiar with her recent career. She even wore the tank top whose stretch knit and pastel look were her trademarks.

But she reasoned that no one was here except a few small boys, come on their bikes from nearby neighbourhoods for a Coke and some chips or candy. It was a weekday morning. She had picked the perfect time. No one would notice her.

Again she addressed the ball. After a moment's concentration she struck it. It sailed over two hundred yards, lofting handsomely before drifting to the weedy grass of the driving range.

In her legs Joanna felt nothing unusual. Her twisting follow-through, though an inevitable strain on her collateral knee ligaments, had not been painful.

Encouraged, she struck a second ball, then a third, a fourth. With each swing she forced herself to put full weight on her convalescent knee. On her sixth shot she went for length. The ball, hit with perfect tempo, sailed over two hundred and sixty yards.

Then she began to guide the ball, fading it intentionally, then drawing it, and finally aiming right for the two hundred-yard marker. With satisfaction she heard her balls whack the wooden planks of the pockmarked sign, far across the littered field.

Directing her attention away from her knee, she hit the entire bucket of balls, then bought another. The tremendous heat of the morning seemed to loosen her. The broken-down old club, whose grip had been taped and re-taped like her own sprained limbs, was poorly balanced, but she knew how to compensate instantly for its deficiencies, and before long it had become an extension of her arms, her back and legs, and she knew precisely where each swing would send the ball.

For the first time in two months she felt in her limbs the coolly professional self-assurance she had taken for granted before her accident, and thrilled to recognise her own talent as it came to life after so long a sleep.

Midway through the second bucket of balls she began to hook her shots. She realised her left knee felt languorous.

Testing the leg, she walked back and forth in the cubicle. The knee was weak and tired.

Wisely, she turned to leave, then she stopped in her tracks.

A group of boys in shorts and dungarees was standing behind the cubicle, the smallest and most raggedy-looking gallery she had ever had.

'Lady,' said a red-haired boy whose T-shirt bore stains Joanna recognised as grape juice, 'you hit the ball just like Jack Nicklaus. Are you a pro?'

Joanna smiled at his candid admiration. 'Thanks for the compliment,' she said. 'But, you see, I'm tired already. Would any of you gentlemen like to finish this bucket of balls for me?'

Eagerly they took the club from her and began taking turns striking the balls with ungainly swings. They all waved happily as she got in the baking jeep and drove away.

The knee was swollen and painful by the time she entered the air-conditioned house. Sighing gratefully in the cool air, she cursed herself for having pushed herself a shade too far when the evidence of strain was already palpable.

Perhaps, she thought dully, she never should have gone out in the first place. But it was too late to turn back the clock.

Reid would be back this afternoon. How could she hide what she had done from his sharp eye?

She thought of the athlete's bible slogan, R.I.C.E.— Rest, ice, compression, elevation. She took two aspirins and gave herself a lengthy ice massage. Then she lay on her bed with the throbbing knee taped and elevated. She prayed it would improve before Reid got home.

After two hours in bed she tried to walk to the kitchen. She could only limp painfully. She tried to eat a snack, but her discomfort and chagrin took away her appetite.

Seeking to pass the time by working on the Black Woods design, she found herself unable to concentrate. The holes danced confusedly before her eyes.

Feeling like a guilty child, she limped ashamedly about the house. At last she slunk down to the basement and sat on the table, as though her proximity to the tools of rehabilitation could somehow strengthen the knee she had managed to harm. Still dressed in her skirt and tank top, she made a pathetic figure in the mirror.

At last she heard the garage door open, heard the

girls rush into the kitchen above as Reid and Virginia brought up the rear, and a moment later Tina came down the stairs.

'Mom!' she exclaimed. 'I learned how to do a somersault under the water. Katie can do it twice. Wait till I show you!'

'Good for you, honey. Did you have a nice picnic?'

As the child answered Joanna saw Reid come into view. His brow furrowed in concern and then disapproval as he stared from her knee to her guilty eyes.

'Why don't you see if Mrs Hughes needs anything?' he said to Tina. 'I want to talk to your mother.'

He approached, touched the knee, flexed and extended it gently, and saw Joanna wince.

'What have you done?' he asked, all business even in his anger. 'Where did you go? The jeep was still warm.'

She looked at him with half-hearted defiance.

'The driving range.'

He shook his head, bitterly amused by her foolishness.

'What did you hit?' he asked. 'A driver?'

She nodded, grimacing anew as he moved the knee through some of the one hundred and fifty degrees of which it should have been capable.

'How many balls?'

'I don't know,' she sighed. 'A bucket and a half . . . maybe fifty or sixty. I don't know.'

'And you quit when you got tired?'

She nodded.

'Did you give it some ice?' he asked.

'Yes.'

Softly his finger traced the skin over the knee cartilage and ligaments, moved the kneecap back and forth, and checked for fluid accumulation as he extended her leg.

'You little idiot,' he grated when he had finished. 'What do you think we've been doing all these weeks? Strengthening this knee so that you can ruin it for ever in one morning? Do you want to go to the U.S. Open again, or do you want to leave your career at a cheap driving range?'

'I'm sorry.' Joanna dared not meet his reproachful gaze.

'Don't apologise to me,' he said. 'It's your career. Look in the mirror and apologise to yourself—or to that little girl upstairs. But not to me.'

Hot tears quickened in her eyes as the pain in her knee joined her guilt over what she had done. But she fought them back, too proud to weep shamefacedly before him.

'I thought I had Joanna Lake here,' Reid went on, 'the consummate professional, the queen of consistency and good sense—not some impetuous child who would jeopardise her own training just because she's in a hurry to play again.'

All at once anger came to Joanna's rescue under his stinging words. She had been under his sway long enough, she decided as she glanced into his hard eyes.

'You're right about one thing,' she said firmly. 'It is my career—not yours. You can break my back all day with your exercise programme, Reid, but when it comes to swinging a golf club on the pro tour, I have to do that myself. No one can do it for me.'

She hesitated, unsure of her own meaning.

'I had to know,' she concluded.

'And now you've found out,' he prodded derisively, 'that you can't drive sixty balls without straining your ligaments and possibly setting your convalescence back by a month or more. Does that satisfy you?'

'Perhaps it does,' she insisted, putting a reluctant arm around his shoulder as he helped her up the stairs. 'But

I had to know if I can still hit the ball. I may have been wrong in going this soon or in staying so long, but at least I did something on my own. And I have only myself to answer to.'

They reached the landing and started past the kitchen towards her bedroom. As luck would have it Virginia and the girls were nowhere in sight.

'It's easy for you to talk,' Joanna went on, limping angrily beside him as he supported her with a long arm. 'You're not the one who has to worry about my future—I am.' She glanced warily around her, alert to her daughter's whereabouts. 'Dr Diehl thinks I'm only good to push a shopping cart for the rest of my life. It's I who have to wonder what's going to become of Tina.'

'Tina won't be better off,' he replied implacably, 'if her mother behaves like a child instead of an adult. A responsible athlete knows how to take things a step at a time—I would have thought you knew that.'

The soft pastel hues of her bedroom came into view as afternoon clouds flashed by in the glass of the painting on the wall.

'I've said it before, and I'll say it again,' Reid concluded with deliberate complacency, 'you need someone to watch out for you.'

'Don't tell me that!' cried Joanna, infuriated by his proprietorial manner. 'I don't need anyb . . .'

'Don't need anybody?' he mocked. 'How would you have gotten up those stairs and down this hallway without me?'

'I'd have managed,' she insisted as he deposited her unceremoniously on the bed. 'I haven't needed you or anyone else all these years, you know. I got where I am on my own.'

Reid stared sardonically down at her swollen knee. 'Yes, I can see that,' he said.

'What's that supposed to mean?' she asked, though his implication was maddeningly clear.

'I wasn't the one behind the wheel the day you got yourself into this, was I?' he asked, his handsome face bent over her in the still air.

Pushed beyond her limit, she stared daggers at him.

I was doing fine until I met you. The words had almost popped out before she could manage to suppress them. She knew how much they would have hurt, for she had no doubt he was aware of the part he had played in causing her accident. But she also knew she had only herself to blame in the final analysis. Provoked through she might be by his arrogance, she could not bring herself to use the truth against him after all he had done for her.

'You treat me like a slave,' she changed the subject irritably. 'It's as though my body belonged to you. I have no rights and no freedom around here. I'm at your beck and call all the time, and when I'm not following your orders I sit around with nothing to do. You leave your instructions and then you breeze out until all hours, doing God knows . . .'

'So,' he grinned down at her, his eyes flashing mockery in the shadows, 'you're jealous, are you? Now I'm really beginning to understand you.'

'Don't you dare say that!' she shot back, beside herself with frustration. 'You think you're the centre of the world . . .'

'All right,' he interrupted, his palms raised in a hands-off gesture as his probing irises rested upon her, and Joanna recognised the odd look that seemed to strip her to the buff while teasing her with the promise not to come too near. But now there was an unaccustomed gentleness in it that disconcerted her. Suddenly she felt too aware of her own shame to be as angry with him as she would have liked.

'You're as stubborn as they come, Joanna,' he told
her, 'and as independent. You'll do exactly as you
please, right or wrong. And for that, believe me, I
admire you.'

He touched her knee for a last time. 'As far as I can
tell,' he said, 'nothing is sprained. The swelling will go
down soon enough. But from now on I want you to do
what *I* say, and not what that strong will of yours
dictates. Is that clear?'

Catching the shade of lingering anger in her gold-
flecked eyes, he shook his head admiringly.

'Damn,' he muttered, 'you are a lovely woman. But
your looks alone won't make you a living.'

Before she could decide what his words meant he had
drawn her to him and kissed her cheek. He held her
closer, patted her back with a protective hand and, on
an apparent impulse, brushed her lips softly with his
own.

'Now,' he said, helping her to lie back while he placed
cushions under her left knee, 'get some rest. I'll be back
after a while.'

A moment later he had closed the door behind him.
The shadows of hot afternoon glowed through the
curtains.

The pain in Joanna's knee was deep and exhausting.
But she did not feel it. Her lips had come dizzyingly
alive, their thrill coursing far beneath her skin.

She lay stunned with wanting in the darkness, her
body on fire, her mind in an agony of indecision.

CHAPTER SEVEN

To Reid's surprise and Joanna's delight, the fateful day at the driving range had been a first step upward rather than a disaster.

The knee felt stronger the next morning, and stronger still the following day. It seemed that one good workout at her actual golf swing, with its graceful follow-through and fluid tempo, had reminded her injured sinews of what their job was. In good order they responded.

Joanna felt surer of herself when jogging and bicycling, when doing quad sets and leg lifts with her weighted boot, and when negotiating her endless Nautilus exercises under Reid's direction. She could sense the end of her convalescence drawing nearer. She was less depressed and irritable now that the day for flying on her own wings seemed a real eventuality.

Her nerves tingled with new strength and vigour as July reached its torrid end. But unbeknown to anyone else, the mad ferment in her senses, stoked to a fever pitch by the sweet brush of Reid's lips the night of her transgression, went on apace. She tried to blunt its urgency by reminding herself that he had only intended to cheer her up in the wake of his own harsh words.

And indeed, since that moment he had been his old self, upbraiding her pitilessly for her occasional failure to comply with his orders, prodding her constantly with the sharp edge of his humour, and bantering easily about her foibles with an amused Tina. He apparently thought she had got off too easily at the driving range, and deserved to be taken down a peg. Yet he was easy and affectionate even in his authoritarian moments.

111

The little signs of his admiration, from his tender handling of her knee to the regard in his sharp eyes when he discussed the Black Woods design with her, were unmistakable and meant a lot. But part of her longed to draw conclusions from his respect that the rest of her knew to be unjustified—and so she continued to suffer quiet agonies alone.

Her sidelong glances, hooded and abashed, caught the hard line of his shoulders, the crisp tangle of hair on the deep chest under the open collars of his shirts, the roguish, sensual curve of his lips. She found herself so close to him that she became expertly familiar with his clean, tangy male scent, the tiny changes flashing across his complex eyes and through his voice to suit his mood. The shape of his hands and fingers was intimate knowledge to her, as were the muscled contours of his thighs and hips.

In guilty solitude she coveted the male energy behind his laughter, and the fascinating variety of his smiles. In his dauntless cheer she no longer saw the superficiality she had once attributed to him, but an almost aesthetic depth of character. There was hard, cold courage behind those blithe smiles and jokes, and a powerful intellect and awesome virility which had perhaps won many uphill battles in life.

It was impossible to be indifferent to him. Small matter if he didn't know she was alive, if his levity covered over whatever awareness he might have of her shameless impulses, and if Tina stood as the crucial chaperone between them. Joanna's senses were full of him at every instant of the day, and his handsome form stalked her dreams at night, caressing and enfolding her as she slept.

She could not get him out of her mind. His intervention in her life, begun with the accident, was now complete. When she looked inside herself to wonder who she really was, and what was becoming of her, it was his black eyes that seemed to look out at her, holding her in the thrall of their knowing gaze.

Yet it was not as a secret lover, a charmed prince, that Reid spoke to her over breakfast a week after her ill-advised day at the driving range. It was as her appraising coach.

'I'll tell you what,' he said, 'Tina is spending the afternoon with Virginia and Katie. Why don't we hang around until they go, and then get in a quick round of golf?'

Joanna's face lit up.

'Reid, do you mean it? Really?'

'We'll go to Bayside Links.' He frowned a warning. 'But we'll play the back nine only. You'll ride in a cart, and at the first sign of weakness in that knee, we're coming straight home. Is that clear?'

She nodded obediently, too overjoyed at her good fortune to ask questions.

Joanna's clubs were still in Florida, so Reid rented her a set at the Bayside Links pro shop. Like so many of Beaufort's genteel inhabitants, the club pro said nothing to Joanna, though his decorous nod signified that he knew not only her identity but also the probable importance of the occasion.

Reid drove the cart to the tenth tee, and they were off. Joanna played her first shots gingerly, and then began to stroke the ball with greater confidence. Her putting felt even more rusty than the rest of her game, but it too improved.

Despite her concentration on her swing she found herself scanning the fine old course's fairways with an architect's eye. It was easy to see that the Black Woods layout, according to her design, would offer women a far more subtle test of golf than Bayside, while assuring male players a championship challenge as well.

Reid, for his part, seemed more intent on Joanna's game than his own, though he drove the ball long distances without apparent effort. He studied every movement of her body, every facial expression that might connote pain or fatigue, and he was alert to the level of concentration with which she attacked the course.

By the time they reached the fifteenth tee he must have been satisfied that she was in reasonably good condition, for he began to put pressure on her.

'The winner gets to skip Nautilus tonight,' he said teasingly.

'You're on,' she nodded, determination quickening under her smile.

They had halved their first five holes at par. Thanks to his natural ability and superior strength off the tee, Reid was able to stay even as Joanna went for birdie after birdie on the closing holes. When they came to the eighteenth green they were still tied. Joanna had uncorked a fairway wood worthy of her international reputation, and her ball lay only ten feet from the cup. Reid gave his own ball a fine roll from thirty feet, and it missed by inches.

'This is your chance,' he told her. 'Make that ten-footer and you're the winner.'

'I'm aware of that,' Joanna murmured as she lined up her putt.

'Good,' he prodded annoyingly. 'Because if I were a professional I'd hate to think I couldn't beat an amateur.'

'May I have a little silence?' she asked in irritation.

'On the other hand,' he drawled, 'I am a man. I suppose that makes a difference.'

Infuriated by his words, Joanna needed an effort of will to turn her anger into disciplined concentration.

With deliberate calm she stroked her ball straight into the cup.

Before she could reproach him for his snide behaviour the sound of enthusiastic applause broke out behind them on the stretch of lawn leading to the clubhouse. A small, informal gallery had formed after Joanna was recognisd on the fairway, and was calling out its appreciation of her putt and its encouragement for her eventual comeback.

'Go get 'em, Joanna!' she heard the friendly shouts, charged with humour and genuine warmth. Though Karen had forwarded hundreds of fan letters to her through the summer, the sight of that small group of boosters touched her, for she realised that her struggle for rehabilitation was not lost on them. Despite the widespread reports that her career was at an end, they continued to believe in her.

With a smile and a wave she bent to retrieve her ball, then shook Reid's outstretched hand. At that instant she heard the click of a shutter, and a photographer came forward from the apron.

'Mind if I use it, Miss Lake?' he asked with a glance at Reid. 'Local folks know you're here, and it would give them a thrill to see you on the sports page.'

She looked at Reid. Smiling, he shrugged.

'All right,' she said. 'You're welcome to it, if you want it.'

'Thanks a whole lot, Miss Lake.' And the man was gone in the dispersing gallery.

'You played a nice back nine,' said Reid. 'That was a good-looking birdie putt just now.'

'Thank you,' she said. 'You weren't much help.'

'Really?' he quirked a mocking eyebrow. 'I thought I gave you the little spark of anger you needed. If you can stay mad at the women on the tour the way you do with me, you'll win everything in sight.'

Joanna shook her head as he helped her into the cart. She could not help pondering the secret understanding that had bound her to him in the wake of her accident. Though he loved to exasperate her, he was her strongest ally; he alone believed in her utterly.

'I can't,' she murmured.

'Can't what?' he asked, his eyes scanning her face.

'Stay mad at you,' she admitted with a rueful smile.

They returned home to find a note from Virginia, who had decided to gratify Tina's wish by taking her to the drive-in movies with Katie. Since it would be late when the show ended, Tina would be allowed to complete her dream evening by sleeping in Katie's upper bunk.

'They have a nerve, to leave us to our own devices,' Reid frowned. 'Well, we'll show them. How about dinner out? Can you use a break from your lean hamburger and cottage cheese?'

'Now you're talking!' smiled Joanna.

After a whirlpool bath to rest her knee, she chose a soft, clinging shift whose simple lines accentuated the femininity she feared she had lost over these painful weeks. It felt wonderful to look at her shapely legs without the cumbersome tape, her slender arms without their black and blue marks and bandages. She saw in the bedroom mirror that her face was truly clear now, and vibrantly healthy. The green eyes looking out at her in the dusky light bore an almost impish look of anticipation that disconcerted her.

Reid met her in the corridor, tanned and handsome in his light slacks and sports coat, his hair still damp from his shower, the clean aroma of him suffusing her delightfully.

'Now,' he took her arm familiarly, 'where's that photographer when we need him? You look like a million, Miss Lake. I'm proud to be seen with you.'

Joanna turned to see herself in the hall mirror, standing beside him in the warm golden glow of sunset. Her breath nearly caught in her throat, for, dressed as they were for a festive dinner out after their round of golf, they looked startlingly like man and wife. Fiddling with an earring to hide her emotion, she realised she had never felt closer to him than tonight.

Reid must have sensed the drift of her thoughts, for he spoke with wistful humour. 'What am I going to do,' he asked, 'when you and Tina go back home and leave me all alone here? Life is going to be mighty dull.' He shrugged unhappily.

'I'm sure you'll get along as you always have,' she smiled, imagining the many women he must know.

'Well,' he sighed, touching her sleek hair with fingers that caressed her neck lullingly, 'a fellow simply has to adjust. I'll make do, but it won't be easy.'

Gently he turned her towards the foyer. The ocean wheeled in the glass frame of an abstract painting on the wall. It was time to go.

And all at once Joanna felt as though they both knew something they had never known before. Yes, she mused as he held the door for her. As though they had come to the last unspoken agreement, their final secret pact.

So it was that the first vodka Martini she had tasted in two months sent shivers of quiet excitement through her limbs. Reid had chosen a beautiful seafood restaurant whose delicious smells harmonised bewitchingly with its subtle décor and massive windows overlooking the shore.

They spoke little as the friendly waiter brought savoury mussels and clams, crab and shrimps and lobster in a magnificent array before fading into the muted background where local people and a few lucky tourists conversed in relaxed tones.

When he returned to refill their wine glasses with chilled white Bordeaux, Reid was watching with satisfaction as his hungry guest enjoyed her un-accustomed feast.

'And how is the Catch of the Day?' came the waiter's caressing South Carolina drawl.

'She seems to be doing very well,' joked Reid without taking his eyes from Joanna.

She could only blush at his humour, for a mood of sweet acquiescence had fallen over them both. Tired but happy, Joanna matched him smile for smile, never daring to look in the face of her own inner feelings, or to hope that she was not alone in feeling them.

They drove home along the coast road in the gathering darkness. The hushed boom of the surf echoed in Joanna's ears, a warm counterpoint to the breeze furling the boughs of the trees in the scented air.

The house seemed familiar and domestic, and not at all its huge, impersonal self, as Reid pulled the car into the garage and led her through the inner door.

She took off her shoes and stood barefoot in the kitchen as he excused himself, and a moment later she heard the low tones of his voice as he spoke on a faraway phone. He must be calling his answering service.

It occurred to her that he might be leaving soon, going out as he did so often to unknown destinations while she stayed home. But tonight Tina and Virginia were gone as well.

Suddenly Joanna felt atrociously vulnerable and even embarrassed, at sixes and sevens alone in the kitchen. She longed for Reid to return, for him to say something, anything by way of setting a tone for the rest of the evening—even if it were only to send her unceremoniously to bed.

At last he returned. He must have thrown his coat

somewhere, for he stood tall and strong in the slacks that hugged his powerful legs, his shirt open at the neck, the very picture of triumphant masculinity at ease with itself.

'Well now,' he appraised her from across the empty room, 'what have we here?'

Pursing her lips in answer to his teasing look, Joanna drummed a finger on her folded arms.

'It seems to me,' he observed, 'that certain people have had a very long day, and should be thinking about a warm bath and a long sleep.'

She stood before him, her weight on her right leg. His acute eyes noticed her posture immediately.

'Now look,' he said. 'She's favouring her weak knee again.' Striding forward quickly, he swept her up by her waist and deposited her on the kitchen counter. The sheer fabric of her shift slid upward along her thigh, baring the knee whose scar was now faded to a tiny speck.

Reid leaned over her, his large fingers closing delicately around the skin he had taped so many times.

'I hope you're not hiding any pain from me,' he said, flexing and extending the knee gently as his eyes followed its movements. 'Because I'm responsible for this little outing, you know. It would be my fault.'

Joanna blushed despite herself as he touched her, his hand so large that it could nearly close around her slender thigh. What she was hiding, she knew, was far more guilty than mere pain. And as he stood before her, his perfect man's body sending its waves of thrilling warmth through her senses, she knew she was perilously close to being unable to hide it an instant longer.

'Does that hurt?' he asked, turning the knee slightly.

Dying inside, she looked up at him, and her heart leapt within her breast as with a great inner sigh she risked everything.

'No, silly,' she smiled, 'it doesn't hurt.'

Her fingers had strayed hesitantly to his hair, languorous but sure, in their way, and caressed its careless waves, felt its fine fragrant expanse for the first time before her hands clasped around his neck. She did not flinch when he looked into her eyes, his gaze sharp with surprise and perhaps disapproval.

She merely smiled, prepared now to stake everything on him, to let herself be torn and ruined if he refused her. The subtle pressure in the cool fingers around his neck told him what she wanted as she pulled him to her with soft entreaty.

And all at once she was in his arms, her body lifted from the counter and pulled full length against his own in one fluid motion. She had no leisure to tell herself how delightful it was to run her fingers through that black hair, to caress those shoulders, to feel the myriad tiny shudders of her femininity against his hard limbs— for already his kiss was upon her, unbearably penetrating and delicious, and she was limp and helpless in his embrace, her courage spent.

Now Reid knew the secret that had tormented her all these weeks. The next move was his, for she had bared everything. It was within his power to take her brutally to her room, to make her his slave there or put her to sleep like a naughty, forward child.

So she clung to him, languid and luxuriant, her senses quickening madly under his touch. Her hands had slipped to his broad back, stroking the muscled flesh with little shocks of delight, slipping down to his waist as her face turned up to his. Again he kissed her, cradling her soft body with a long arm while he furled and caressed her billowed hair. His lips joined her own with exquisite gentleness.

A wild joy took possession of her, for she could feel the acquiescence in his warm hands, his willingness to accept what was about to happen, and even to protect her, as he always had, from her own doubts.

The dark night wheeled before her half-closed eyes as he bore her through the shadows to her room. He deposited her with ethereal delicacy on the silken spread. There was moonlight in the window, and the walls shone silver and iridescent around her. It seemed there was a hushed, secret sigh of compliance in the darkness itself, a conspiracy of yielding that opened her senses to him.

Stunned, she lay that way until his kiss made her sit up and strain towards him. She felt knowing palms slide over the body whose injured sinews they had comforted for so long. Dry and calm and concerned, they caressed her. But now she trembled in her very centre at the hot ferment they stoked under her skin, the shudders of ecstasy their passage coaxed from her.

Already her shift had slipped away somehow, and in the quiet rhythm of Reid's touch her underclothes were coming off, stripped slowly away with all the grace of petals in the breeze.

Naked, she watched as he stood up in the penumbra. Outlined against the glimmering wall, he removed his clothes and stood in his stately nudity, huge and straight and handsome as she had always imagined he would be. Joanna held out her arms to him.

Enthralled to feel him cover her, his hard bands of muscle melded flawlessly to her woman's curves, she realised in breathless excitement that she had never wanted a man so terribly, never dreamed of a pitch of desire so feverish as this.

Reid seemed to sense the transport that shook her, for he was kind and tender as he gathered her to him. Her hips and thighs and stomach awoke to the touch of his hard flesh, her breasts to the lithe stroke of his lips and tongue. And she knew now that this unearthly pleasure was all new, blissfully unfamiliar, for she had never been made love to like this, never known so sweetly and perfectly.

She felt the surge of his enormous heat, and was unashamed to feed and excite it, for she had nothing to fear now, and was certain of it. She touched him and led him, delighted to feel him respond to her with his aroused power as her soft limbs surrounded him. Hard and potent, he gave himself to her as surely as he had given her his smiles, his teasing looks, his harsh commands and encouraging words all these weeks.

Now the great swell of his need upraised her, thrust her higher and higher, and she gave him all of herself gladly, her hands in his hair and upon his broad back and on the taut thighs beneath his waist. Her sighs and murmurs enfolded him, and she heard the low groan of passion stir in his throat as he kissed her and held her, closer and closer, his hard essence joined to her in hot bursts of pleasure unimaginably intense, unspeakably intimate.

Then all was poised and breathless on the edge of peace while their passion spent itself in the shadows. Reid cradled her and did not let her go as her gasps softened to little sighs and shudders in his arms. The hands and lips that stroked her cheek, her breast, so sweet and gentle, told her something she felt she could hold on to for ever, no matter what the future held.

She knew now that he was perfect for her, had understood her utterly and given himself just as she wanted him, in that wondrous, charged moment. He had come from nowhere to enter her life, to change her and make her perfect for him, so that in this silent darkness she might experience the thrill of being known so beautifully.

And if he had come to her thus, only to recede into his own destiny, then so be it, she thought with a little spasm of defiance. Let time take him away, and humiliation descend upon her. He was hers tonight.

And perhaps he felt her wild opening to him, her heedless willingness to confront fate that way. For, a warm and steadfast partner, he joined her in her defiance, he stayed with her all night long. They lay somnolent in each other's arms, charmed by the moonlight, caressing each other softly until passion rose to draw them together once more. Both knew that this lovely tryst might be their first and last, and so they discovered each other again and again, in surprise and delight and rapture.

How many times she belonged to him that night Joanna would never know. Each intimacy she shared with him was stunningly unique, too beautiful to ever recapture or forget. The varieties of his tenderness were indescribable.

And when at last sleep came to bind them, in the night's darkest hour, after the moon had set, she knew she was a changed woman, and would never be the same again. But she could welcome the awful vulnerability inside her, the fearsome yielding help-lessness, because he had stayed with her, and even now held her in his arms. Surely the magic of that embrace would give her strength to go on alone when he was gone.

One perfect night to hold off the entire future.

Joanna had known equations more improbable.

CHAPTER EIGHT

SUMMER was ending.

There was no denying it, despite the blazing August heat that kept tourists and residents at the beach or indoors. The calendar did not lie. Soon the migratory birds would depart with the human visitors, leaving the graceful herons and egrets to their year-round home. The famous golf courses, booked up now for tee-off times, would return to their placid off-season tempo.

It seemed that a great pressure had been lifted from Joanna's life—at least for the moment. By dint of innumerable knee lifts, quad sets, and stretching exercises for her back, hamstrings, hands and arms, all under Reid's stern aegis, she had restored her body to the strong, supple condition she had taken for granted before her accident.

Since their historic first round together, she had played golf with Reid when he was available, and alone or with young Katie Hughes when he was not. Gradually abandoning the use of electric golf carts, she now tramped eighteen holes of fairway with vibrant confidence in her stamina.

Having pronounced her latest examination in Charleston the last, Robert Diehl considered Joanna to be entirely rehabilitated, though unfit for professional competition in the sport she now pursued as a hobby.

Joanna alone knew that she could play the game of golf from tee to green as well as she ever had. She found she could compensate for the predicted residual weakness in her left knee through judicious use of tape to restrict excess motion, along with a minor

124

adjustment of her swing. The great test of competition in exhausting four-day tournaments against top pros would have to wait, of course, until next spring.

That left a long fall and winter of conditioning and mental preparation. Though impatient to play again, Joanna was resigned and philosophical about the months ahead. One season, after all, was not too much to sacrifice to convalescence in the wake of so serious an injury.

The Black Woods design, meanwhile, had reached its final, strikingly original form. All eighteen holes were finished and clearly sketched in their definitive positions relative to the ocean and hills around the layout.

'What happens now?' Joanna had asked the night she presented Reid with the finished product.

'I'll submit it officially,' he told her. 'There will be meetings. You may be called in to explain a few things. These people will need to be reassured that this is a championship layout, and not just a crazy idea.' He shrugged. 'But I'll do whatever arm-twisting is necessary, even though it may take time. You've done your part. The design is perfect, unbeatable. When it's all over, there'll be a contract, and of course a fee— which will make up for some of the tournaments you've missed this summer. Then you'll relax until you get your next commission.'

His dark eyes bore the look of intent, brooding concentration she had often noticed when he scanned the design or talked about it. She realised that his own contribution to its future might involve subtleties of business acumen, perhaps of persuasion and compromise, whose importance he preferred not to mention.

Joanna's eventful and challenging summer in Beaufort had served its productive purpose. After the trauma of the accident, which left her feeling broken and hopeless, the process of healing had joined the joy of creative inspiration in repairing her physically and mentally.

Clearly the moment was at hand for a confident return to Sarasota, where school would soon begin for Tina and a variety of business obligations awaited her mother. There were dealings with her agent, her insurance company, and the staff at Nakoma Springs to take care of, along with taxes and correspondence and a score of other duties which had kept Karen Gillespie from her novels and her boy-friend far too long.

The shimmering summer seascape of Beaufort County, with its Golden Islands and cloudless skies, must now take its place among the many images in Joanna's crowded memory. There was no reason to stay here any longer.

She should have been delighted to get on with her independent future after so lengthy a hiatus, but instead she was torn by emotions more painful than anything she had experienced in the darkest hours after her accident.

It seemed that she and Tina had barely had time to accustom themselves to the routine of life in Reid's house before it was hurtling towards its end. And a peaceful, sweet routine it had been, its daily rhythm punctuated by Joanna's spartan exercise and Tina's outings with Katie when Reid was away on business. The two girls walked the nearby lawns and pastures together or swam at the beach within sight of Virginia's kitchen window. Occasionally Joanna would look beyond the bridle path at the end of the lawn and see them crabbing together in the sand, their pails by their sides.

As luck would have it, Tina was sufficiently precocious to relate easily to her older playmate, though Katie's maternal instincts, without an outlet at home, might well have cemented the friendship in any

case. Her father having died years ago, it fell to Katie to
send her older brothers off to their summer jobs and
close the house before coming 'the back way' to Reid's
kitchen door. Joanna soon discovered herself to be high
in the pantheon of the young girl's adored heroines, and
had to nudge her gently into accepting her as Tina's
mother and a merely human adult.

The hot summer days had passed in gentle
uniformity, their customary schedules broken occasionally by special events which hung pleasantly in Joanna's
memory. There was the night Reid took everyone to see
a revival showing of *Gone with the Wind*, which he knew
to be Tina's favourite movie. And there was the day
Joanna had taken her bicycle to meet Reid and Tina for
a picnic lunch at one of the crossroads linking the bike
trails and bridle paths. The three had eaten their
sandwiches under the bored eyes of the tethered horses,
much to Tina's delight.

But most of all there was the warm familiarity of life
together. Reid, more than ever a figure of almost
paternal dependability in Tina's eyes, presided over the
background of her adventurous world while not
hesitating to discipline her on the rare occasions when
her little transgressions merited it.

He read with her every night, and came to know the
entire range of authors who absorbed her imagination.
He was privy to her observations about her teachers
and friends, and knew her intention to become an
author of children's books when she grew up.

When Joanna watched them together she felt the
trust and mutual respect that underlay the interplay of
their personalities. Tina's implicit confidence in Reid
shone in her manifest contentment as she sat on his lap,
held his hand or toyed with the buttons on his shirt.

But it was impossible for Joanna to contemplate their
closeness dispassionately, as though she herself were not

involved in it. For her fantasy of life as a family with
Reid, which had so tantalised and disturbed her when
their summer together was just beginning, now seemed
a reality that was all the more magical for remaining
unseen by the outside world.

Indeed, if Tina experienced a daughter's secure sense
of belonging with Reid, then Joanna herself possessed
the precious essence of life as his wife.

Their opportunities for privacy were rare—a stolen
afternoon in Charleston, an evening in Atlanta after
Joanna had consulted a sports kinesiologist there—but
somehow they sufficed, along with the occasional
moment at home when she could let her feelings show
in the green eyes that rested on Reid's face or in the
hand that touched his own.

Denied a wife's free access to her husband's caresses,
denied even the little hugs and casual kisses which are
the public signs of a young couple's affection, Joanna
nevertheless felt joined to Reid by a bond whose
mysterious power exceeded anything she had imagined
possible in her wildest dreams about marriage.

Perhaps, she mused, it was the very difficulty of this
shadowed communion with Reid that made its
accomplishment so special. When they were together in
Tina's company, or with Katie and Virginia, they
bestowed their tenderness on each other in a language
so covert, so indecipherable to anyone but themselves,
that Joanna felt its subtle essence, light as a whisper,
like a charm that penetrated with almost occult
difficulty to her heart.

She already knew Reid's perfect male limbs, the
variety of his scent, the salty taste of him on her lips.
Now she knew the complex eloquence of his silence,
and the gentle support he communicated through the
most offhand of words and glances.

In his palpations of her knee, a scarcely necessary

precaution nowadays, there was a calm memory of the intimacy he had shared with her silken skin. His way of holding a chair for her, or of brushing a windblown strand of hair from her cheek, was no less redolent of the quiet knowledge they could not but hide from those around them.

For her part, Joanna found herself shaken by a thousand inner thrills when she reflected that the hands that grazed her hair, her shoulders or her knee in these everyday moments, knew every inch of her, and had set her every sinew aflame in their passage, not so long ago.

She could still see herself, naked and suffused with desire, reflected in the tawny eyes that smiled down upon her now. And she saw Reid's body in a new light, as flesh dedicated to her own and united with it—for underneath his open collar she knew the clean hard line of his pectorals, the lean descent of muscle under his chest to his stomach, where crisp hair descended in a little whirlwind shape towards the lithe sinews beneath his waist.

Without shame she had known those beautiful contours of pure virility, caressed and coveted them as though they belonged to her. And Reid, who knew where she was damaged and hurt and vulnerable, who had seen her at her worst, Reid had accepted her and wanted her. As he gave her ecstasies of unbelievable fulfilment, his embrace was tender and knowing, as though she were indeed his, had always been and would always be his own.

So it was with private exultation that she felt herself enfolded by a warmth which was all around her every day, as though she were truly married. Alone in her bed at night, she seemed to nestle still in Reid's arms.

It was bewitching, that private tryst conceived in silence and yet so real, consummated in plain sight and yet unseen by anyone. But Joanna could know its joys only at the price of its inevitable pain. For neither she nor Reid had spoken of love, or even of the future. The understanding they shared was in another dimension— intimate, no doubt, romantic and even heroic, but necessarily doomed.

Acutely aware that she had made the first move towards him when she could cope with her desire no longer, Joanna could not bring herself to lay the slightest claim to Reid. He was a man who had already conquered his freedom at a cost and a risk known only to himself, and she knew his life was his own.

Joanna was both a harsh realist and a dreamer. She was no stranger to impermanence and insecurity, and could accept them as facts of life. Her struggles in an often unfair world had accustomed her to coping with disappointments, losing illusions, and standing on her own two feet. But she also retained traces of belief in the gentility and propriety handed down from her Southern forebears by Paul and Ellen Lake.

In her mind, love and marriage did not overtake one in the dizzy manner of her affair with Reid Armstrong. Women did not throw themselves at men the way she had done. No, love and marriage had a more stately and traditional tempo and mood, which included hesitant probings, sincere statements of frank admiration, promises made and kept.

Reid was the opposite of these things. He respected no tradition and accepted no status quo. He lived without strings, and believed in nothing but his own initiative.

'I'm a businessman,' he had told her often enough. 'I pursue my own advantage. If it dovetails with someone else's, we both come out ahead.'

From the beginning he had made clear that his relationship with Joanna was a business association based on mutual self-interest. His obvious respect and esteem for her did not change that fact.

And now, consenting adults, they had indulged in a physical involvement which had no meaning and no importance. Having initiated it herself, Joanna could hardly harbour any illusions about it.

Reid was far from the marrying kind. Having accepted him thus, she knew both the peace and the despair of her intimacy with him. She welcomed what she had of him—his humour, his friendship, and her memories—and forced herself to see in his calm silence not only the obvious understanding that their relationship involved no commitment and no permanence, but also his awareness that she considered him free and made no claim on him.

And perhaps, she told herself, perhaps the quiet tenderness in his dark eyes bespoke his gratitude for her renunciation.

She hoped so. She wanted to be strong for him, and to justify his confidence in her. Thus he would never know what her courage would never reveal: that he had changed her life for good in this brief summer. His smiling image had penetrated to the most private corners of her past and future, and could no more be dislodged than her soul could be torn from her body.

She loved Reid, and she would always love him.

Now, at last, he had lost his Cheshire Cat ambiguity and coincided with himself—in her woman's heart, where he belonged and would forever remain. And Joanna, true to his promise and his commitment, had healed and grown vibrant and supple again—but her new persona was like a vine twined around his hard limbs. It was through him that she had come to herself, healthy and strong and exultantly full of her need for him.

And now, because she must use that precious strength to let him go, to give up the one support that made her feel like a whole woman again—now, suddenly, she did not feel whole.

With a shrug that concealed a breaking heart, she resolved to do what was necessary and inevitable.

School would begin in Sarasota during the last week in August. In the reluctant way that visitors and vacationers have, Joanna and Tina scanned the calendar and chose a date for their departure. From that moment on life could no longer go on as before. It was sadder and less carefree, for it was under the shadow of its end. One felt one was going through the motions of an existence that had seemed so real and solid only days before. The beaches, trees and pastures, and even the horses, had a halo of impermanence about them.

Now they must leave this beautiful, impersonal house where Reid had come to rest in the midst of his life's peregrinations three years ago, this house he hardly considered his own. And a terrible thought told Joanna that he, too, might be leaving it soon, selling it when it ceased to amuse or profit him, and moving forward into a future as inscrutable as his past, a future far from this time and place.

So that the house, handsomely anonymous, would be like those holiday cottages and resorts whose empty rooms contained the ghosts of people who had met and shared romance there during the charmed days of a long-ago summer that had seemed endless until it had been inevitably cut short by time.

And here she would leave a part of herself that she could never regain.

In the last days before their departure Reid was bright and humorous as ever, whether through bravery or simple tact Joanna could not tell.

'Just think,' he told Tina, 'you'll be a fourth-grader now. The younger kids will be scared to death of you. How do you reconcile yourself to being an Embarrass-King yourself?'

'Oh, I can reconcile myself,' said Tina, snapping up the adult word with ease. 'Because Suzanne will be with me, and if Suzanne can be a fourth-grader, anyone can.'

'What about Lynn and Allie and Abbas?' he asked.

'Well, they'll be there, too. But I'm just sure that Susanne will be in the same class and reading group with me,' she explained, articulating her fond hope as though it were a certainty.

Joanna's heart was breaking as she watched them together. Tina had never had a father. The only male presence in her life had been Carl Jaeger, a distant grandfatherly figure who sent her birthday cards and spoke to her on the phone at Christmas. With uncomplaining courage she had lived as a child of divorce. Joanna had suffered to see her spend afternoons and nights with friends who had fathers, and had even taken miserable comfort from the fact that, with the divorce rate as high as it was, Tina knew more than a few children in the same predicament as she, and so could feel less alone.

But Tina had taken to Reid so naturally and beautifully, planting her roots in the rich soil of his friendship. And now this gift that had been held out was to be taken away. It was a cruel thing for her little heart to bear.

They must both leave the tall, vital man who had presided over their summer with such blithe assurance. And each, in her own way, must go on living as though he had never crossed her path. But there was no turning back the clock, no sewing the heart shut, no erasing the memory of him from the mind and soul.

The morning of their departure dawned bright and still. Over a quiet breakfast Reid spread his cheerful humour.

'Here,' he said, placing wrapped packages in front of

both of them. 'I want you two to have something to remember me by.'

Tina unwrapped her box to find a cuddly teddy bear whose golden fur would set it apart from any other in the collection Reid had often heard her describe.

'I think I'll call her Sandy,' she said, instantly taming the new acquisition and determining its sex.

'Go on,' Reid pointed to the small box before Joanna.

Inside it was a tiny gold charm on a chain, in the shape of the slogan '#1'.

'Thank you, Reid,' she said, barely able to return his wry gaze.

'Remember, now,' he said, 'this is part of our agreement. I told you I'd see to it you came out of this mess better than new—and I always mean what I say. You won't really be through with me until you're a winner on that L.P.G.A. tour. Unless you get out there and bring home the first-place money you deserve, you'll have me to answer to. Is that understood?'

With the kindest smile she had ever seen, he put the charm around her neck. Fighting back her tears of joy and anguish, she nodded her obedience to his warning. She knew she would happily lose a thousand tournaments if it meant he would come back to her.

But he would not come back. The goodbye in his eyes was real, and there was no point in pretending she had not seen it.

So she clung to the little charm as a final sign of his admiration, forcing herself to banish the forlorn hope that it might mean something more. As his warm hands brushed her shoulders she resolved for the last time to accept what she had of him, even if her sacrifice meant permanent exile from her very self.

Moments later they were outside in the driveway beside the new car Karen had left for them to bring home. In the back were Joanna's clubs, their suitcases, and a large bag containing the books Tina had brought with her or acquired this summer.

'You'll take care of your mom for me, won't you?' asked Reid, sweeping Tina high in his arms for a last hug before he put her down. Nodding her yes, she kissed his cheek.

Then it was Joanna's turn. His arms encircled her back with quick, friendly warmth. Hesitantly she returned his embrace, not daring to show her emotions in front of Tina. Her slender hands lingered for a split second on the hard flesh beneath his shoulders, alive with a message too frail to reach its destination, for time had run out.

Torn by the impotence of wanting to tell him so much, and knowing she could not, must not, she met his eyes with a last smile, then turned away.

The new station wagon purred softly as she edged it along the drive leading down to the road. The distant beach lay vacant beyond the bridle paths at the base of the lawn. A hushed repose seemed to have descended upon the sea and sky.

A sudden impulse made Joanna look into the rearview mirror before turning on to the roadway. She saw Reid standing before the house, his arms at his sides, watching her recede from him perhaps for ever.

Unable to bear the sight for more than an instant, she looked quickly back to the empty road spreading before her. But as she did so she caught a glimpse of Tina crying quietly into the fur of her new teddy bear.

Pridefully the little girl turned away to look out the side window, wiping at her eyes with a small hand as she avoided her mother's gaze.

CHAPTER NINE

As September approached it seemed that survival from day to day was all that counted. The fragile ray of hope which persisted under the banality of the hours was mentioned neither by Joanna nor Tina.

Their attractive but modest ranch home on its quiet street seemed singularly dull after Reid's palatial ocean-view house. But its familiarity was comforting.

Tina went about her business with the mute endurance of childhood. The only sign that something was wrong was her failure to call Suzanne. Apparently unconcerned to anticipate fourth grade under her new teacher, she closeted herself with her dolls and books, or moped sluggishly about the house. Joanna could only hope that the natural resiliency of her age would see her through.

But they were both changed; there was no denying it. Joanna could not suppress the feeling that her time with Reid had been a strange dream, begun by the brutal accident and ended in the bitter-sweet confusion of summer's end.

But if it was a dream, she reflected, it had left more than its share of palpable scars in its wake. For so many years she had taken pains to depend only on herself. Now she knew the awful strangeness of needing and wanting a person who was no longer there. The void inside her could not be filled or ignored, and she knew it was haunting Tina as well.

She still had her knowledge that Reid would be in touch with her about the Black Woods design. He had promised to call or write when there was news. One day

136

soon she might actually see him, if only on business. Perhaps they would have dinner together, or spend an evening . . .

She cut off her girlish hopes with a shrug of impatience. Any illusions she might harbour about Reid Armstrong could only make things worse at this already difficult time in her life. Forcibly reminding herself that his gentle goodbye in Beaufort had signified nothing more than a friend's affection, and perhaps the discomfiture of a sometime lover who feared her dependence on him, she put him firmly behind her.

There was nothing to do now but get Tina ready for school and endure the winter. Joanna enrolled at a nearby Nautilus centre, began practising her golf, and did her best to take an interest in her agent's suggestions for her immediate future.

She knew she must wait until next spring to find out whether she had a future at all in her profession.

So long to wait for news that might be bad . . .

One day she was in Sarasota shopping with Tina for school clothes. In a half-hearted effort to cheer the child up she had brought her to a favourite fast food restaurant for lunch. They were ready to leave when an oddly familiar voice addressed her.

'Hello, Joanna.'

Though she knew the face looking down at her, she could not place it at first. Its elegant lines were a bit harder than she recalled. Harder and heavier . . .

Then it hit her.

It was Jack—Jack Templeton.

She nearly laughed to think she had not recognised him. He was her ex-husband and the father of the child who now sat beside her, toying with an uneaten French fry.

The child who had never known him.

'Tina,' she said, fumbling in her purse, 'would you take these quarters and see if you can win something for yourself back there?'

With a curious glance at the stranger Tina took the coins and moved towards the video arcade adjacent to the dining room.

'Sit down,' invited Joanna, clearing away the loose wrappers on the table top. 'I'm sorry it's such a mess.'

'Just for a minute,' he smiled. 'I'm on my way to a meeting, but I noticed you and thought I'd say hello.' There was something unpleasant in his demeanour as he sat down before her. In his hand was a rolled-up magazine. 'I'd heard about your injury, but I saw a picture of you on the golf course in the sports pages the other day. I hope you're feeling better.'

She nodded vague assent.

'Did you meet Reid on the golf course?' he asked abruptly.

Taken aback, she recalled that the photo of her with Reid on the eighteenth green at Bayside Links had been sold to a wire service, and had appeared in newspapers all over the country. If Jack had recognised Reid, that could only mean he knew him already—as his casual first-name reference to him certainly suggested.

'Not exactly,' she said. 'I met him before my accident. We had a business deal together—some golf architecture.'

'Black Woods,' he nodded, leaning his heavy frame against the moulded plastic booth. 'Sorry about the way it turned out.'

Thunderstruck at his words, Joanna allowed her gaze to stray over the lines of his face and body. He wore an impeccably tailored suit, light and handsome, the jacket thrown over his arm in the noon heat. She could see that he had gained some weight around the middle, which accentuated the aura of prosperity about him. She had forgotten how tanned he was.

Though he still seemed powerfully muscled, her athlete's instinct told her he was out of condition. There was a trace of dissipation in him, but she lacked the practiced eye which might have linked it to alcohol.

'How did you know about that?' she asked, unable to conceal the candid vulnerability of her words.

'I'm on the board that's financing that club,' he explained. 'And on the course committee, in fact.' He twisted a bit uncomfortably on the narrow seat. 'Naturally I was disappointed for you, but I'm afraid the result wasn't unexpected.'

A sinking feeling came over her as she fought to return his gaze without flinching. She knew now that this meeting was no accident. Jack had come here in search of her. He intended to hurt her. Deep underneath her present fear she even thought she knew why. She recalled having heard somewhere that his second marriage had ended in divorce several years ago, without providing him with the son he must have desperately wanted.

In his slightly twisted features she saw the weak, angry man she had divorced. He must be lonely, and frustrated by his failure to give his father a grandson. He had seen Joanna's photo with Reid.

And now he had seen her with his own daughter, whom he had never met.

But these thoughts were a mere flash at the back of her mind, pushed aside by her certainty that he possessed a weapon capable of hurting her seriously. The triumph in his dark eyes left no doubt of it.

'I don't understand,' she said, screwing up her courage.

'Well,' he said, pretending to hesitate before discussing an unpleasant topic, 'I mean the committee's decision. Naturally, I voted for you, being prejudiced.' He laughed sheepishly. 'But it was all a pro forma exercise. You couldn't get such a revolutionary design past a bunch of fogies like that even if it was done by Jack Nicklaus—much less by a woman.'

He raised an eyebrow in feigned perplexity. 'Funny,' he added.

'What do you mean?' she asked.

'Well,' he said, 'when that vote took place—and of course the result was a foregone conclusion—I couldn't help wondering why Reid would encourage you to do such a crazy thing. After all, as the finder he knew what sort of group he was working for. That's pretty conservative golf country—I've been on several boards of directors in that area over the years, and I know.'

Joanna recalled that Jack's only real profession was inheriting his father's financial responsibilities. Jack was the custodian of the family name on various boards of directors, and as such oversaw the progress of his father's investments. It came down to the role of an enormously wealthy errand boy.

'The whole thing didn't make sense,' he concluded, avoiding her eyes. 'Unless . . .'

'Unless what?' she asked, anxious for him to show whatever weapon he possessed.

'Well,' he said uncomfortably, 'this is a bit embarrassing, Joanna. How well do you know Reid?'

'Not well,' she said, reminded by the chill of dread inside her that this lie had more than its grain of truth. In fact she did not know Reid well at all.

'He's a bit of a ladies' man,' said Jack, his smile of distaste distancing the observation from himself.

'I'm not sure I follow you,' she returned.

'Forgive me,' he went on implacably, 'but you're considered one of the beauties of the ladies' tour. Deservedly so, of course,' he smiled. 'If Reid took a liking to you, he wouldn't want to take no for an answer. I know him. He stops at nothing when he takes a shine to a girl. He'd take advantage of his finder's position to offer you that commission, even if he knew there was no chance in hell of your proposed design being accepted.'

'You're presuming a lot,' Joanna said tonelessly.

'It does sound crazy,' he drawled. 'I couldn't understand why you'd undertake such a hopeless thing. I thought I knew you to be levelheaded to a fault. But I told myself that Reid is after all a handsome devil. He can put quite a rush on a female.'

He glanced at her knee, which was lightly taped for the long shopping walk.

'Of course, I didn't consider your injury. It happened just about then, didn't it?'

His probing enraged her, for she alone knew the role Reid had played in controlling her convalescence after the accident he had had a share in causing. But she contented herself with a noncommittal nod.

'Well, it doesn't matter,' Jack sighed complacently. 'I do hope that, at the right time and in the right place, you can make a name for yourself as an architect. I suppose it was good experience, even though it seems cruel of Reid to have let you go through with finishing the whole damned thing.' He shrugged. 'Maybe he just wanted to be able to tell you he had submitted it, and to blame the result on the committee. 'Or,' he quirked an eyebrow, 'perhaps he thinks he can sell it somewhere else. He's not the sort of man to throw away an advantage. He'll kill two birds with one stone if he gets the chance.'

He was reaching into the inside pocket of his suit jacket.

'This might interest you,' he said, handing over a letter in a business envelope.

'What is it?' she asked.

'Just to show you how cheap these committee

members can be,' he shook his head in disapproval. 'They hired an expert to evaluate your design. But it was a hatchet job from the beginning. They picked a fellow who could be counted on to assassinate the design, once he knew it came from a woman.'

Joanna had to force back the tears welling up in her eyes as the curt letter opened before her.

'Clever, innovative,' the words flashed up at her, typed in large pica figures. *'Unfortunately,'* the letter went on, *'the plan shows both inexperience and self-indulgence.'*

'An unfair test of golf for both sexes,' she read at the bottom of the page.

The letter was signed by Carl Jaeger.

'Funny,' Jack was saying, 'I thought Carl was so high on you. But I guess some things are even bigger than friendship. Too bad,' he pursed his lips sadly.

Joanna could neither speak nor look at him. She fought to regain her composure.

'Well,' he went on, 'with Avery Follett as architect the course will be what they want: old-fashioned as they come.' He touched the magazine he had with him. 'It's already in the Announcements,' he said. 'I suppose Avery can't hurt the land too much.'

Avery Follett was a well-known golf course architect whose designs were predictable in their workmanlike, unimaginative contours. Joanna recalled bitterly that his courses were uniformly unfair to women players.

'When did all this take place?' she asked, cursing herself for revealing her ignorance. 'This meeting . . .'

'Oh,' he rolled his eyes towards the ceiling, 'it must be a couple of weeks now.'

Joanna stared straight at him. Though deeply hurt by his blows, she had recovered her sense of perspective.

'You came a long way to tell me all this,' she said. 'Have you said all you wanted to say?'

It was his turn to avoid her eyes. 'I thought someone should warn you,' he shrugged.

She took a deep breath.

'How are your family?' she asked.

'Oh, fine,' he replied uneasily. 'Mother and Dad are after me to get married again, but I tell them three strikes and you're out.'

A small hand on Joanna's wrist tore her intelligent eyes from his face. Tina was standing beside her.

'Mom,' came her decorous whisper, 'I'm bored. I don't like those games. Can I take my book outside and read?'

'No, honey,' Joanna smiled. 'We have to leave.' Unceremoniously she rose and took Tina's hand.

'Give your parents my best,' she said to Jack. 'Nice of you to say hello.'

She saw him turn away in sour triumph as she left the restaurant.

An hour later Joanna found herself alone on the beach looking out over Siesta Key to the Gulf of Mexico. On the sand beside her was a copy of *Golf Journal*, whose Announcements column indeed bore news of Avery Follett's nomination as course architect for the Black Woods Country Club in Beaufort, South Carolina.

Beside the magazine was a cardboard mailing tube. Inside it was Joanna's copy of the Black Woods design. She had addressed the label to Reid Armstrong before leaving home. Karen, seeing the look in her eyes, had quickly agreed to take care of Tina until her return.

She had stopped here to think before going on to the Post Office. But rational thought would not come. Isolated midday beachcombers and sailboats passed unseen before her eyes. Only anger and hurt swirled inside her head.

Like all cowards, Jack Templeton had waited to strike

until he knew his victim had no defence against his weapons.

'Perhaps it was good experience,' he had said in his triumph.

She shook her head bitterly. After all she had learned, all the joyful inspiration and imagination and excited effort she had poured into that design, she knew now it had never had a chance. Her strange and beautiful agony of self-discovery had been for nothing.

Her work had been done in a void created by Reid's treachery. And it had all happened because her accident immobilised her, taking her away from the summer tour and making her vulnerable to a proposal she would never have had the time or inclination to accept otherwise.

All because of the accident, which itself had resulted from Reid's arrogant invasion of her life, and from her own stupidity . . .

And now her life, so calm and controlled only three months ago, was in jagged pieces she would never be able to put together again.

Thanks to Reid.

'All for nothing,' she thought.

Rendered violently alert by pain and humiliation, her mind darted past all the scenes of her summer-long relationship with Reid, and focused without pity on damning images whose significance she had never questioned before.

I'm a great fan of yours, he had said that first afternoon after her loss to Peggy Byrne at Pine Trail. *But I'm here in a business capacity.*

The cleverest of liars, he had used his salesman's aggressiveness to get his foot in the door with her.

I'd like to ask you a historical question. How many of the championship golf courses in this country were designed by women?

She recalled the mocking way he had stood aside to let her pass in the corridor beside the Pine Trail locker room, and his irritating claims that she was afraid of her own ambitions.

How would you like to be the first?

It would be a great step forward for women.

The tones of his cajolerie haunted her, alternatively provocative and lulling.

I think you're even prettier in person than you are on television.

'My God,' she thought, reddening with shame, 'what a fool I was!'

Reid had tried every trick in the arsenal of a handsome, seductive man. He had appealed to her vanity, to her personal ambition, her creativity, her social consciousness as a representative of women in golf—and even to her anger. Where his other blandishments failed, his psychologising remarks about her loser's mentality had succeeded in getting under her skin.

And she had been attracted to him from the very beginning. Why deny it now? She could still remember her solitary bath the night after the Pine Trail tournament. His face, so devilishly handsome, had haunted her thoughts no less than his tempting proposal.

And he must have sensed her response. He must have known he had a chance with her. He was probably calculating his next move when the providential accident occurred, landing her in his clutches for an indefinite period. From that moment on he must have realised he had only to stay close to her, flatter her, keep her busy and, in his own subtle way, play hard to get. Prolonged contact with his physical charms would do the rest . . .

One advantage remained to make his ascendancy

over her complete: the affection of her fatherless daughter. He had quickly covered that ground while Joanna lay unconscious in her hospital bed. By the time she had awakened to her pain and helplessness, Reid had make all his arrangements for her convalescence, and made his promises to Tina . . .

And now, three months later, that innocent little girl was preparing to enter fourth grade with a painful void inside her little heart. Thanks to Reid.

As though she had not suffered enough already in her young life.

Cold fury overtook Joanna now as the image of the exploiter crystallised around Reid in her mind. Perhaps Jack was right, she thought. Having set out to seduce her for his own amusement and satisfaction, Reid might well have been impressed by her talent as an architect, and might even now have vague plans to sell the design, or its principle, elsewhere.

He would kill two birds with one stone if the opportunity arose. That was his nature.

Now she understood the brooding look that had come over him whenever he studied the design. It was a look of calculation and cunning. Always aware of its inevitable rejection, he had to plan his own actions with that fact in mind.

When he could avoid submitting the design no longer, he had done so. It had been refused, of course. He had instinctively avoided telling her the truth about its fate until he could think of a way to let her down easily, to convince her that he was not responsible for the committee's decision, that all was not lost . . .

So that he could keep her on a string, keep her happy, and perhaps condescend to dally with her when his business took him to Florida or when he felt bored or lonely . . .

For he certainly did not have to worry about her

attachment to him. Had she not thrown herself at him shamelessly the night he took her out to dinner after their round of golf? The mad pitch of desire in her soft limbs must have been pathetically obvious to him. As was the girlish, romantic cast in her eyes as her sidelong glances betrayed her dependence during those last weeks of the summer.

And at this very moment he was probably busy somewhere with someone else, his thoughts turning occasionally to Joanna Lake with musing concern. He must take care of her somehow, and keep her available while making sure that her starry-eyed possessiveness did not become a problem.

I'm a businessman. I always pursue my own advantage.

Yet, as she touched the gold charm around her neck, her eyes on the mailing tube beside her, it was not Reid that she blamed for the cloud of misery that had descended on her life. It was herself.

Thanks to her own flawed instincts where the opposite sex was concerned, her beautiful daughter had been born of a doomed, futile marriage, and scarred by a fatherless childhood. And now the child had been hurt yet again, her hopes raised and dashed, thanks to her mother's irresponsible and idiotic behaviour.

With a deep breath Joanna brought her thoughts under control. What mattered now was not Reid. He was out of her life. She must decide what to do.

She would earn nothing from the design she had spent the summer working on—that was obvious. She had won no money this season, after the Southern Invitation. She had bills to pay, and precious little income to pay them with. Should she sit on her hands, dry her tears, and count her pennies all winter while waiting for the uncertainty about her profession to be ended when next year's tour began? Should she try for the hundredth time to put her manifold failures behind her, and look prayerfully to the future for better luck?

The answer came to her as she stood up, dusting the sand from her skirt. She hurried to the post office. After a moment's thought she took the '#1' charm from around her neck, threw it in the tube with the design, and mailed it.

Then she went to the nearest pay phone, gave the long-distance operator her credit card number and her caddie's phone number in Arkansas.

'Robbie,' she said, grateful to hear the mountain twang of his familiar voice, 'are you working for anyone next week?'

'No, Joanna. Just building a porch with my brother.'

'Can you meet me in Ithaca on Sunday?' she asked. 'The Tournament of Champions will be held there next week, and I'm eligible to play without qualifying. Take your motorcycle, or a plane if you want. We're going to play that tournament.'

Hiding whatever perplexity he might feel, Robbie agreed without comment, and Joanna hung up the phone with a deep sigh.

In her present mood the sole course of action open to her was obvious. She had made an irremediable mess out of her personal life, and could expect no one to come to her rescue. The future depended on her own initiative, which had been reduced to practically nothing by events she could not control and people she had naïvely thought she could trust.

But she could still swing a golf club. No one could do that for her, or stop her from doing it if she chose to.

The odds were against her, and she knew it. But fourteen years of training and experience would guide her when she faced this most difficult of tests.

Determinedly she walked towards the lot where her car was parked. She was alone now, and ready to act alone on her own behalf. Her solitude would have been almost comforting had it not been for one persistent thought which hammered underneath her resolve, though she dared not put it into words.

If Reid had lied about the Black Woods design, perhaps he had also lied when he said she would play golf again.

CHAPTER TEN

SHE was not surprised when the doorbell rang the night before her flight for Syracuse.

She had just put Tina to bed. After a glance into her room she went through the kitchen and opened the side door.

In the moonlight Reid stood before her.

'What are you doing here?' she asked, unafraid to unlatch the door so she could see him clearly. The involuntary tremor in her stomach irked her, for she would not allow herself to be afraid of him. She was ready for him, and had been for hours and days.

'I think you know that,' he said. 'You haven't answered my calls, and I'm sick of talking to Karen when it's you I want. So I came.' His eyes gleamed in the moonlight. 'I got your little package,' he added.

After a moment's hesitation Joanna slipped through the door and closed it behind her. She intended to handle him out here and get rid of him. Tina would never know he had been here.

The half-moon spread silvery light over the lawn and flower beds. Crickets added their thrum to the soft stirring of leaves in the breeze.

'Well,' he said, 'I'm waiting. What happened to make you send me the design that way?'

For an angry instant she contemplated him. His severity was clearly a ruse designed to keep her attention. He was a salesman, a wheeler-dealer who hated to take no for an answer. He would do anything in his power to retain some sort of influence over her. The only sure way to defeat him was the strategy one used with all salesmen: to simply refuse to argue with him.

'Reid,' she said, mastering her emotion with difficulty, 'listen to me. When I've finished you can say whatever you wish to say, and then I want you out of here. I know the design was rejected. I know the commission has gone to Avery Follett. I know what you did in Beaufort, and,' she sighed, 'I know why. As far as I'm concerned, our business together is finished. If you have any sense of pride, you'll walk away from here.' She thought for a moment. 'That's all,' she concluded.

Despite herself she recoiled an inch as the shadow of his tall form covered her in the moonlight. His eyes seemed to bore into her, aroused and flashing.

'You saw that little item in the *Journal* about Follett, didn't you?' he asked. 'What did you do? Put two and two together?'

She shook her head, not wanting to join in the dialogue he wanted to initiate. She knew he would argue anything, deny anything, say anything, just to keep her talking.

'The details aren't important,' she said curtly.

'You never learn,' he sighed. 'I've told you and told you to leave the business end of this whole deal to me. I'm a professional at this, as you are on the golf course. I don't know who's been putting ideas into your head . . .'

'Reid,' she cut him off, 'why do you go on? Why don't you just leave? Why don't you leave me alone?'

'Because,' he said, staring down at her from his terrible height, 'for one reason, I want to peel the scales from your eyes. And for another, I have a business relationship with you that is too valuable to drop.'

'No,' she nodded, revolted to think of the male needs he undoubtedly had in mind along with his financial plans, 'I'm sure you don't want to drop it.' She folded her arms. 'But my word is final. Keep the design. Do whatever you want with it. Throw it in your garbage can in Beaufort if you want. Paper your bathroom with it—I won't have anything more to do with it!'

There was perplexity in his gaze, as well as suspicion—or the pretence of it. Joanna told herself she must take none of his words or gestures at face value. In two minutes Reid would be gone, having feigned anger or hurt or who knew what before he finally gave up. She must merely survive those two minutes.

'Listen to me,' he said, 'before you jump to conclusions. I didn't tell you about the Follett business for two reasons. In the first place, it wasn't important. In the second place, I didn't want to worry you about it when you had other things on your mind.'

'Not important!' cried Joanna despite her resolve. 'It seems to me it was a yes or no situation. The answer was no. Someone else got the job, Reid. What else is there to say? Have you no honesty?'

'Your job,' he persisted, 'was to conceive the design. Mine was to see it through with the committee. Why don't you let me do it?'

His words amazed her. He would say anything to cloud the issue.

'Do with it what you wish,' she said. 'But leave me. Please. Now.'

'Don't turn away from me,' he warned, his large hand closing around her arm in a grip which was not without its hesitancy, as though he were afraid to jerk her backward for fear of hurting her injured body.

Yet there was infinite urgency under that softness, and she was shocked to feel sensual flares of responses quickening inside her as he held her motionless in the cool night air.

'I need to know,' came his deep murmur, 'that you're all right.'

'That's wonderful!' She whirled in his grasp, wrenching her arm. 'Well, don't worry your head about it, Reid. You put me up, helped me train, and kept me busy all summer—in more ways than one. I owe you a debt of gratitude. But all good things must come to an end.'

'What's that supposed to mean?' he asked.

'You only did what came naturally to you.' The cruel words sprang from her lips with a harsh eloquence that surprised her. 'You did what your instincts told you to do. Well, that can cut both ways!'

He stared at her, genuine surprise vying with the anger in his eyes.

'You're fond of calling yourself a businessman,' she told him, seeing that she had hurt him. 'You got what you wanted. And I'm back on my feet now. Our relationship was mutually beneficial, and now it's over. Why beat a dead horse with your lies?'

'Lies?' Reid's hands closed around her arms. 'So you don't believe me.'

Her flowing blonde hair outlined by the moon, she shook her head, refusing to look at him.

'I wonder when I've ever given you occasion to doubt my word,' he said. 'I'm not going to let you get away with this.'

'That's rich!' she said bitterly. 'How can a person who's nothing to me decide that he's not going to let me get away with something? You're out of my life. The next time you see me, if ever, will be on television.'

'And you'll have me to thank for that, in part,' he said.

'I have you to thank for the fact that I was injured in the first place!' Joanna spat back, losing control of herself. 'You knew it all along—you practically said it yourself. It's thanks to you that I may never compete again. Thanks to you, Reid. Now haven't you done enough?'

She knew her cruel shaft had struck home. An enormous rage seemed to seize him, more at himself for having armed her thus against him, than at her for plunging the dagger.

'So that's how it is, then,' he grated. His voice was low, menacing.

'Yes,' she said, beside herself with anger and guilt. 'Unless you'd like to get Tina out here and see what she has to say. She might be willing to take your side. She doesn't know you, after all, as I do. You've done a great job of winning her confidence. She has no reason to think badly of you, does she?'

Joanna felt a horrid escalation of emotion in the soft night air between them, more and more violent, and she had the awful presentiment that everything was about to come out, including the feeling she could not banish in herself whatever her pain, the feeling that continued to fuel and spark her very cruelty, binding her to him despite herself, making her want to hurt him as he had hurt her, so that he could not forgive her or forget her, ever, ever.

And Reid must have sensed what was truly behind her slashing, furious words, for he silenced her with a kiss so intimate, so brutal and penetrating that she felt her whole body tense in an unforeseen spasm of excitement against the maddening hardness, the electric virility of him.

Pinioned by his mouth no less than by the iron grip of his long arms, she gasped in ecstatic consternation to feel her squirming, twisting limbs forced closer and closer to him. Already their struggles were alive with a lithe and slippery animal pleasure she could not quell. He was coaxing it from her, that soft rhythm of female yielding, and she could not think how to stop him.

A mad paroxysm of anger and delight shook her all at once, deep and uncontrollable, and she could only shudder in his arms, limp and defenceless and unforgiving.

At last he released her, gentle in his triumph.

'So,' he said, 'we both had our fun. Is that it? We passed the time together. And that was all it meant to you.' His low voice was cruel, painful in its intensity.

'Yes,' she said, to silence him, to banish him. 'Yes, that's what it meant.'

A moment later she found herself alone in the shadows. The half-moon was rising fast, spreading pale rays across the sky. She heard the distant throb of a motor, the thump of a big car leaping into gear.

Then nothing.

Nothing. The word was fearsome, sending creeping tendrils of emptiness through all the most vulnerable corners of her soul.

A first sob shook her in her solitude. A pang of weakness shot over her knee as she sank to the cool grass. She knelt there, her tears flowing unchecked, in the darkness outside the house where her daughter slept.

And now it seemed that the whole world had receded from her, leaving her alone here in the darkness and the silence, with no companion other than the ironic, romantic moon, rearing above her like a mocking symbol of her final failure in love.

For what seemed an eternity she sat alone, her hurt leg extended beside her. Her hands touched the tender grass under the magnolia tree. She contemplated the sweet indifference of the balmy night, hovering over her like an old acquaintance, a mute witness.

She knew Reid would not return. She had pushed him too far, hurt him as he richly deserved to be hurt. Now he was gone, having no doubt understood in his cold heart that she was not buying what he was selling. He had turned tail and gone, his sharp eye in search of greener pastures.

And taken her heart with him.

With a sigh Joanna raised herself to her feet and moved through the night towards the screen door. It closed quietly upon her slender form.

CHAPTER ELEVEN

'LADIES and gentlemen, your attention, please.' The announcer's voice resounded among the gallery massed around the first tee at Maple Hills Golf Course. 'Our next threesome will include Sandra Noble, from Rochester, New York . . .'

Appreciative applause greeted the attractive young professional, who had won her first tournament only two weeks ago, and thus qualified for today's event.

'Yvonne Shelby, from Canton, Ohio . . .'

The popular veteran of ten successful pro seasons smiled her acknowledgment of the crowd's applause.

'And Joanna Lake, from Sarasota, Florida.'

A small ovation erupted, tight with suppressed emotion, as Joanna tipped her cap to the gallery. The TV cameras zoomed pitilessly to her left knee, which had been taped by Robbie this morning.

'This is a dramatic and touching moment for Joanna's many fans,' the network commentator murmured. 'Some observers have questioned her decision to play this week. She has not, of course, won a tour event this year. But the official rules of the Tournament of Champions allow the holder of the previous year's Vare Trophy to compete regardless of whether she has won in the last twelve months. Joanna holds that trophy, as she has three times in the last seven years, and so she has decided to play. But the primary concern here today is her physical condition. We may be seeing the last hurrah in a great career, and there's the risk of permanent injury if that left knee is subjected to too much stress. There are those who think

Joanna should have retired immediately after her tragic accident. But here she is.'

No one gave Joanna a chance in the tournament, and she knew it. Her participation was a human interest story, spiced by the familiarity of her lovely face and figure and the visible signs of her injury. The press was already making hay out of what it saw as her mad eleventh-hour attempt to salvage a wrecked career.

'What makes you think the knee is ready?' one of the reporters had asked after her practice round on Monday.

'I think it's ready,' she had replied simply.

Then it had been Ron Lieber's turn.

'How do you expect to beat a field like this, all tournament winners, coming off an injury like yours?' Clearly he was irritated to see her competing at all, since he had announced her retirement in his column a month before.

'I'll do my best,' Joanna smiled noncommittally.

Charlie Sullivan, the oldest and most respected member of the group, added his question.

'Since her victory over you at Pine Trail, Peggy Byrne has won the Salem Classic and finished second three times. She seems to be at the top of her game right now, and this event undoubtedly represents her last chance this season to win her fiftieth tournament. I think it would be safe to say she wants this one badly. It will be awfully hard to beat her, won't it?'

'You're telling me,' nodded Joanna, her candour bringing appreciative laughter from the journalists.

Oddly enough, it was Peggy herself who had offered something more than the wanly sympathetic words of encouragement Joanna had been hearing from fans and fellow professionals all week.

'Don't let them get you down, Jo,' she had said in the locker room, her plump hands on Joanna's shoulders.

'They had me dead and buried when my kidneys gave out, but I didn't give up. And you won't, either. I know what you're made of. You're no loser, and you're no quitter.'

The sincerity in the older woman's sparkling eyes was as real as Joanna's certainty that she would give no quarter on the golf course. Peggy was a battler and a great sportswoman.

But her encouragement could not wipe out Joanna's fear that she was indeed taking a desperate chance by playing this week instead of resting through the winter. She felt tender and wounded inside. There was no guarantee that the stress of a four-day tournament in the company of the tour's very best players would not force her to push herself too hard.

Even the choice of golf course was anything but propitious, she reflected. Maple Hills had always been bad luck for her. She had been in contention in at least half a dozen tournaments here over the years, and had been defeated each time by the course's great length, its famous, unpredictable wind, or her own poor play in crucial situations.

Somehow she always found herself plagued by nagging little injuries such as backaches, sore wrists or cramped legs when she played here. Once she had even come close to being struck by lightning when a sudden storm interrupted her round.

Maple Hills was not Joanna's favourite course. Yet its long fairways, lined by tall trees in the hills high above Cayuga Lake, were handsome to look at and made an intriguing challenge. She enjoyed passing Cornell University's beautiful campus on the way from her hotel, and found the changeable summer weather of western New York a bracing background for competition.

Her three practice rounds with Robbie confirmed

that the course was as straightforwardly difficult as ever. Only drives and fairway shots of extreme accuracy could produce birdie possibilities on its long par fours. The even longer par fives and short, heavily wooded par threes were less difficult, but if the dreaded wind became a factor, as it always seemed to on at least one day of every tournament here, every hole became a formidable enigma.

The brisk walk over the hilly terrain had tired Joanna's knee considerably, and she had had to rest it in an elevated position every night. She had shown Robbie how to tape it so as to offer her a modicum of support during play, but she felt compelled to give it copious ice massages after every round.

Meanwhile she did elaborate stretching exercises for her back, legs, neck, wrists and fingers. She ate lean meats and fish, baked potatoes and vegetables without butter, apples and melons, and drank only skim milk and fruit juice, eschewing the black coffee she adored. Her mental exercises were as disciplined as her physical efforts. She worked on her concentration and prepared herself for the inevitable ordeal of managing her game and the golf course under stressful conditions.

There was weakness in her knee—of that there could be no possible doubt. The trauma to her collateral ligaments and cartilage had left its mark. It could not incapacitate her, but, in Dr Diehl's baleful phrase, it threatened to damage her confidence in the knee, and thus to take the competitive edge off her play.

If she let it.

That was the challenge, she decided as she played her practice rounds and worked out on the driving range and putting green. She must compensate for the weakness in her knee. But at the same time she must put her trust in it, and believe that it would support her.

Thus she must avoid hitting down at the ball, trying

to scoop it off the ground or guide it upward. She must swing away smoothly, her natural rhythm unhampered by fear or pain. But at the instant of follow-through, when her body's turn twisted the left knee outward, she must make a minimal adjustment in her mechanics so as to take some of the pressure off the injured joint.

If she succeeded she would hit straight and play effectively, although she would lose a small amount of distance on her drives and fairway woods.

If she failed, her journey here would have been for nothing, and the premature end of her career would be staring her in the face.

She knew the odds were against her, for she had not had time to refine the thousand little subtleties of tempo, timing and equilibrium that made up her deservedly famous style as an athlete. Her body was not in optimum condition, and she lacked the sharp competitive instincts her rivals had honed over the long season which was now reaching its peak.

But inside her a cold concentration, born of anger and loneliness and hurt, told her she would not give in. She was alone and vulnerable, but darkly determined to use every trick she had learned as a professional.

Initiative was hers. No one could take that away from her. Permanently scarred she might be by injury and by her own mistakes, but now she was where she belonged: on her own and in charge of her destiny.

The threesome in the fairway had moved out of range. The gallery on the first tee watched in silence as Sandra Noble teed up her ball and stood at address. Applause followed her compact, efficient swing.

The butterflies in Joanna's stomach were uncontrollable as Yvonne Shelby took her turn. The quiet veteran sent a picture-perfect drive down the fairway and picked up her tee with a nod to her fans.

Joanna's moment had come. She could feel the affection of her many supporters filtered through the massed galleries, the press and the network cameras. But even more, as she swung her driver in a soft arc over the grass, shifting her weight gently from one leg to the other, she could feel resignation and incredulity in the millions of eyes focused on her.

She was not the woman whose consistency had amazed the golf world for seven years. They all knew it. Tina and Karen knew it, too, though they had accepted Joanna's decision without protest.

She was not whole, and everyone could see it.

And somewhere the man who had had a hand in the event that had crushed her body might well be watching her. The man she would never see again, but who had taken a piece of her heart with him when he abandoned her to her solitary fate.

She would never be whole again.

But she would do one thing. She would play this round of golf today; nothing and no one could stop her.

A thrill of excitement pumped her up as she addressed the ball. Oblivious to the hush of the concern that had descended over the gallery, she glanced quickly down the green corridor of fairway between the trees.

Pain be damned, she thought as she raised the driver high in the air. *I'm as ready as I'll ever be*.

She brought the clubhead down.

But in that split second she had favoured her weak knee. The ball hooked left, out of bounds, as the gallery sighed its disappointment. Observers looked at each other significantly as Joanna Lake took a double bogey six on the par-four opening hole at Maple Hills.

After the first two rounds the Tournament of Champions was deadlocked. The hungry field of top pros was playing well in perfect weather conditions.

Four women were tied for the lead at four under par, and six others were within two strokes.

The eyes of the golf world were on Peggy Byrne, who had followed her brilliant opening sixty-nine with a lacklustre seventy-three, and stood within striking distance of the lead. Everyone expected her to make a move during Saturday's round and be in contention for the championship on Sunday.

Joanna Lake, having played the first round in a shaky seventy-five after two double bogeys on the front nine, and the second round in seventy-five as well, was written off as well out of the hunt, for the leaders were in ten strokes ahead of her.

Peggy Byrne did not disappoint her millions of supporters. Loose and confident in the crisp, still air of Saturday afternoon, she shot a stirring sixty-eight which tied her for the lead at six under.

A brief shot at the beginning of Saturday's network broadcast showed Joanna in the warm sun with her patented tank top and wrap-around skirt. Her ponytail identified her instantly to the audience, as did the taped knee which was now an unwelcome feature of her screen persona. The commentator made sympathetic comments about her mediocre but courageous performance, and intimated that she might well be playing her last televised tournament.

Their commercial instincts piqued by the human interest potential of Joanna's losing battle against a crippling injury, the network executives ordered their director to give her more air time. With her soft features, her shapely legs mutilated by the tape, and her eyes showing a touch of pain, she projected an almost ethereal beauty that hypnotised the galleries watching her.

Thus it was that the attentive cameras focused admiringly on her tanned limbs as she putted out on the eighteenth green in the shadows of late afternoon.

Yet that final putt, to everyone's surprise, was for a four-under-par sixty-eight and a brilliant third round.

Unbeknown to anyone, Joanna had made a desperate, last-ditch adjustment in her game after a long, meditative bath in her hotel room on Friday night. Her tempo on backswing and follow-through had been rushed as a result of her insecurity over her injury. By slowing her swing and distracting herself intentionally from the tired feeling in her knee, she thought she could correct her mistake.

She ran the risk of tiring the knee further, and perhaps re-injuring it. But her pride would not allow her to play ineffectually before millions of viewers. The long winter of inactivity yawned before her. Beyond it, perhaps, lay a future without golf. She must perform well this weekend.

The strategy had worked, for her sixty-eight on Saturday was impressive and solidly executed, though she remained far behind the leaders.

'If only I could have played three rounds of sixty-eight!' she cursed herself aloud that night.

That's always what a loser says, she mused suddenly, her eyes riveted to the tired face in the mirror.

Sunday morning dawned cold and windy in the hills above Ithaca. Cayuga Lake sat slate grey like a huge puddle in the valley below. As Joanna ate her solitary breakfast, the network director and commentators were planning a series of inserts throughout the day's broadcast to show highlights of her distinguished career. Having seen the effect of her image on viewers during the third round, they wanted to add drama and ratings to the tournament's closing holes by speculating loudly that this heroic fourth round might be Joanna's last championship effort.

Despite her slacks and windbreaker Joanna could feel

the bite of a chilly breeze on the first tee. A scheduling mix-up had put her in a threesome with Peggy Byrne and her co-leader, Linda Sherwood. Though she felt out of place with two players who were doing so much better than she, there was nothing for it but to play her best.

After calculating the strength of the wind she addressed her ball and swung.

'We may not see her again,' the commentator whispered, 'but no one will forget the sight of that wonderful, fluid swing over so many courses these past seven years. And the courage she has displayed this week certainly goes beyond winning and losing.'

The ball sailed two hundred and twenty-five yards and floated to the ground in the centre of the fairway. Robbie took her driver from her as she stood back to watch her partners hit.

'Sixty-four will win it,' she heard him murmur. He looked away as she turned towards him in surprise. In six years she had never heard Robbie say a word on the course except to announce her precise distance from the pin.

He thinks I can win, she mused, amazed by his confidence.

Moments later they had started down the fairway. Too late, an urgent message was handed to one of the marshals on the tee. It was passed along from marshal to marshal throughout the day, but in the confusion of the final round somehow never reached Joanna.

The gusts that shook Maple Hills were even worse than anyone had anticipated. They blew perfect drives into fairway rough and bunkers. They blew accurate approach shots off the greens, and almost immediately the entire field began to lose strokes to par.

Only Peggy Byrne seemed able to stand up to the

ravages of the wind and cold, thanks to her natural strength and shotmaking ability. She kept her ball within bounds, made difficult putts, and finished the front nine at even par for the day. She was already alone in the lead, for her competitors had been unable to keep up with her pace in the inclement weather.

A curious sidelight of the broadcast was the outstanding performance of Joanna Lake, whose image was seen often since she was paired with Peggy. Not only was she striking the ball with surprising authority, the commentator noted in his sympathetic voice, but she had managed to set up several easy putts for birdie through fairway shots of uncanny accuracy.

At the end of nine holes she had actually gained four strokes on par, while everyone else was struggling just to stay even.

Of course, that did not mean she was in contention. She remained four strokes off Peggy Byrne's pace, and the back nine at Maple Hills was known to be even more difficult in the wind than the front nine. Nevertheless, it was said, she deserved credit for her improbably fine play.

At the tenth tee Robbie took a can of fruit juice from Joanna's bag and watched her drink it while he massaged her knee. His rough hands were gentle and hesitant on her soft flesh as he murmured words of encouragement in his Arkansas drawl. She knew he had seen the slight limp she had developed over the last few holes; she had noticed it herself on the fifth.

Too early, she thought.

But already her mind was far away from the present moment. Eyes closed, she was sailing over the tenth hole, the eleventh, and the entire back nine, floating mentally over the fairways and on to the greens in the gusting wind, making shots she knew she had to make.

She knew that angry wind; it had beaten her here

before. In her mind she contemplated it now with respect. It was a rippling, excitable sort of creature that hovered above the trees, slapping at anything that invaded its element, including golf balls.

One must not fight it, she decided. One could only lose, as she had done so many times before. Instead, one must collaborate with it, acknowledging its dominion over this hilly ground. One must offer it one's ball with a certain humility. Thus propitiated, the wind itself would do the rest.

'You've got 'em, Joanna,' Robbie was saying. 'You can't lose!'

She nodded without hearing.

It was all Peggy Byrne could do to salvage par on the tenth hole by one-putting the green after a stupendous pitch-and-run that had the chilled gallery cheering madly.

But before she could make that four-foot putt, Joanna, who was away, sank her sixteen-footer for a birdie. Surprised applause greeted her fine effort.

On the par-three twelfth hole, Peggy could no more hold the green in the whistling wind than anyone else, and had to save par through a brilliant approach chip and ten-foot putt. Joanna, having driven her ball to within eight feet of the pin with a brisk five iron, sank her putt easily for another birdie.

By the thirteenth tee the TV cameras were no longer focusing on Joanna for the hurt knee hidden by her slacks and for the probable end of her career. She was alone in second place now, a respectable contender at two strokes off the lead.

The par-five thirteenth would normally have offered a player of Peggy's strength a tempting birdie opportunity. But today the savage wind made its narrow fairway seem almost non-existent. Forcing her shots from rough to rough, Peggy again saved par through a clutch putt that broke frighteningly before dropping.

Joanna was on the green in regulation and one-putted from twelve feet for another birdie.

The galleries buzzed with excitement as she passed. Somehow, inexplicably, she seemed to have harnessed her own determination to the caprices of the wind, married her ball to the flowing grass and heaving tree limbs of Maple Hills. Her shots charged through the air above the fairways and floated to the greens as though guided by huge, invisible hands.

Slow as always to appreciate an unseen change in the momentum of a tournament, the commentators realised Joanna was in line for victory only when her ball lay on the sixteenth green, a dozen feet away from a birdie that would tie her for the lead with Peggy.

Joanna slammed the putt straight into the back of the cup.

In sixteen holes of golf on one of the most difficult courses in the Northeast, in the cruel wind that made that course so famous a beast, Joanna had gained eight strokes on par. The leaders who had been so many strokes ahead of her this morning were now far behind.

Even as the stunned gallery at the sixteenth erupted in applause at Joanna's putt, an electric hush seemed to come over spectators and journalists alike. They watched her slender limbs in awed fascination as she picked her ball out of the cup. The change in the cold air was palpable.

She's going to win, they were thinking.

If the wind and the course and her injured knee had not slowed her thus far, nothing could stop her now.

Except Peggy Byrne.

Alone in their tie for the lead, Joanna and Peggy both

played the seventeenth hole in par. The network
cameras had ceased bothering to cover the play of any
other competitors, for it was obvious that one of these
two would win.

'One can't help being reminded today of the epic
struggle that was joined between these two women only
three months ago at Pine Trail,' the commentator said.
'That day it was Peggy Byrne who came out on top,
thanks to an amazing bunker shot on the final hole. If
she wants to win her fiftieth tournament here today, she
may need just such heroics to do it, because Joanna is
applying tremendous pressure through her superb play.'

His words struck a chord in a million minds, for
Joanna's awesome rush to the lead from a great
disadvantage had obscured the one flaw in her game
that might offer encouragement to Peggy's many
supporters: her reputation as a loser.

If Peggy could not beat her, she might yet beat
herself.

The eighteenth hole at Maple Hills is as famous a
finishing par five as exists in the United States. Its
slowly curving fairway, five hundred and eleven yards
long, leads past huge bunkers and a transversal creek to
an elevated green protected by a water hazard and
thick, encroaching rough.

Joanna's booming drive sailed two hundred and forty
yards before landing in perfect position short of the
creek. Despite her reputation for great strength off the
tee, Peggy could only manage a far shorter effort. Her
careful second shot left her a seventy-five-yard wedge to
the green.

Robbie's hand flirted with the one-iron in Joanna's
bag. A conservative and accurate second shot seemed
the logical choice for Joanna. But she asked for her
three wood.

'It looks as though she's going to go for the green,' the commentator said as her image appeared on the monitor before him. 'It's a gutsy thing to attempt in this wind, but no one is forgetting that Joanna has been considered the premier fairway wood player in the world for years now.'

Before addressing the ball Joanna glanced at Peggy, who was waiting with her caddy. For the first time she noticed the lines in Peggy's face, and realised that the older woman was nearing the end of her great career. The freckles and laughing eyes and frizzy hair beloved of millions of fans could not conceal the onset of middle age.

No wonder Peggy wanted her fiftieth title so badly, Joanna thought. Time was running out for her.

Distracted by the depressing thought, Joanna lost her concentration for the first time. She hooked her powerful three wood into the thick rough rimming the distant bunker which guarded the green. Had it flown straight, her ball would be on the putting surface. As things stood, her ambitious effort might well have done more harm than good.

Cursing her lack of concentration, she watched Peggy seize the advantage by lofting her easy wedge shot in an arc that dropped her ball no more than ten feet from the cup.

'That rough Joanna is in,' said the colour commentator, 'is far worse than the sand itself. She's going to have terrible footing, and the ball will fly. Meanwhile Peggy will be putting for birdie, and if I know Peggy she'll put everything into that stroke.'

Suddenly the unseen flow of emotion in the galleries seemed to have changed direction. Having played with almost inhuman efficiency all day, Joanna had not only silenced the network's doomsayers, but had made Peggy's scrappy wind play appear frail and ineffectual.

Only moments ago improbable victory seemed sure to go to the younger woman, for her icy nerves and aggressive shotmaking were putting unbearable pressure on the popular veteran.

But now is was Joanna's turn to show the soft, vulnerable face the public had admired for seven seasons.

'It looks as though Peggy will pull out her coveted fiftieth today after all,' the announcer said, 'despite this amazing challenge by Joanna Lake, who seems indeed to be running out of gas now. I don't see how she can stop that ball of hers on the green. As soon as it hits the surface it's going to run all the way to the front edge, and she'll have all of sixty feet coming back.'

Alert to the slight limp that was visible despite her wind-whipped slacks, the camera watched Joanna approach the bunker's edge. Her taped knee twisted painfully as she addressed the ball, one foot in the trap and one foot in the thick grass of the rough. Only the cold wind sighing in the trees broke the silence as the press and gallery contemplated her.

Joanna hesitated, looking from her half-buried ball to the flag-stick forty feet away. She knew she faced an almost impossible shot. Many times as a professional she had found herself in positions like this, had shrugged and made bogey, and hoped for birdie on the next hole, the next round, the next tournament.

But today there was to be no next hole.

She could feel the millions of eyes fixed on her, still tense with anticipation and yet convinced now that she was the loser. They were all waiting for her to overshoot the green, to miss the huge putt or chip coming back, to congratulate Peggy on her birdie and her fiftieth victory.

Her fingers were numb on the grip of her wedge. Her legs and arms were chilled by the wind, and her left knee ached alarmingly. But she felt nothing except that eager waiting, that imminence on the edge of resignation.

The marshal, his demeanour imperial under shiny grey hair, kept the gallery back as Joanna stood poised to swing. She could feel the force of a collective will urging her to get it over with.

They can't hit it, she thought darkly. *They have to wait for me to do that.*

And suddenly a thought rose and flowered in her mind. She looked down at the ball. It seemed joined by invisible threads of force to the gusting wind and the bent grass of the green. Between her and that impossible sixty-foot putt from the front apron lay the hole itself. She had only to stroke the ball directly into the cup in order to avoid disaster. She had only to execute this one unlikely stroke, the stroke of a lifetime, to beat the only woman who had offered her a bit of true encouragement during this terrible week, the valued friend whose fiftieth tour victory was at stake.

A stroke to defeat her.

Joanna raised her club quickly and struck the ball. It popped crazily into the wind, hesitated for what seemed an eternity, and floated to the green, already a pace beyond the flagstick. But she had somehow managed to stun it with a backspin which jerked it suddenly up the slope, backward against the grain and, with a finality that left the gallery stunned and breathless, into the hole, into the bottom of the shadowed cup.

Even the glib commentators were at a loss for words to describe the reality visible on the monitors. Peggy's birdie putt was irrelevant now. Joanna had won the tournament outright.

Seized by an abrupt wave of weakness, she felt oddly embarrassed by what she had done. Pain and languor made her touch her taped knee as she climbed out of the trap. She wanted to meet Robbie's friendly eyes, to hand him her wedge and stand out of sight somewhere as Peggy holed out before the appreciative crowd.

But Robbie had receded from her and blended into the mass of people who were standing up. Deafening noise confused her, and she turned in disorientation to see if Peggy was going to putt out.

But Peggy was standing in the centre of the green, her putter under her arm, smiling as she joined the thousands of spectators in the standing ovation that had exploded under the cold sky, and that grew now in power and intensity until it seemed to drown all thought under its crashing weight.

Joanna could not believe her eyes and ears. The spectators, marshals, greenskeepers and journalists were all on their feet, applauding and calling out words of praise and affection, their thousands of smiles resting as one on her slender form.

Flushing in her amazement, she started across the apron to take her ball from the cup. She wanted to tip her cap to the cheering multitude of faces, but all at once she was afraid the slightest movement would make her lose her balance. The putting surface reared before her, and she felt faint.

It was Peggy who came to her rescue, supporting her with a strong arm around her shoulder and guiding her to the cup in which her ball nestled against the pin. Men with hand-held cameras hovered near her as she retrieved it and threw it to the gallery.

And now Peggy stepped back a pace, and Joanna stood alone before the public, realising at last that the full force of that exultation was for her. Through eyes clouded by pain and fatigue she smiled her acknowledgment, waving and blowing kisses of thanks for the tide of warmth and sympathy that rose and rose before her.

She saw hundreds of index fingers raised skyward, proclaiming that she was Number One, the very best of the very best, for today at least. And she knew now that countless fans had waited and worried with her as she fought to save her career, and perhaps waited and hoped long years for this moment when the spotlight would belong to her at last.

Joanna Lake, said the unnecessary graphic under her familiar image on television screens in forty countries.

Winner.

CHAPTER TWELVE

JOANNA would remember that day as a chaos of her own making, a maelstrom which must surely engulf her unless she could find its hidden principle in the tangled forces of her whole life.

She came to herself blinking and confused before a welter of lights, cameras and microphones. Peggy's plump arm was around her shoulder once more, for she had putted out and was receiving her second place winnings.

'We're all sorry that either of you great players had to lose,' the commentator was saying.

'Not at all,' Peggy laughed. 'For seven years I've known that Joanna was going to do this to me some day. And now that it's happened, I'm just glad I was here to see the round of golf she played. I lost to the best—and that's a privilege.'

'Joanna,' said the tournament chairman with the inevitable prosaism of those who congratulate winners, 'you played a truly historic round today. How do you feel?'

She tried to think of something light and tactful to say, but the words would not come. She realised her reserves of energy were completely drained.

'I ... I guess I'm a little tired,' she said at last, her weak humour sending waves of sympathetic laughter through the crowd. Before she could continue she felt a weakness in her left leg so sudden that she nearly fell down at his feet. Only an enormous effort of will kept her upright, and she had to grasp his arm outside the cameras' view to steady herself.

He must have sensed her extreme weakness, for he resumed with alacrity, 'I'm sure that's no wonder. Coming back from knee surgery the way you have, in one summer, and beating a field as great as this one, on this difficult course in the wind—that's an achievement that won't soon be forgotten. And I want to add my congratulations to everyone else's on one other point, which our viewers may not have heard about yet. I understand that, as well as being the winner of the Tournament of Champions, you've made history in another way today. You've been officially selected as architect for the Black Woods championship course in South Carolina. That's a great step forward for you personally and for women in golf.'

Everything else he said was lost on Joanna. She struggled to mumble responses to his questions while her mind raced ineffectually to comprehend his tidings.

It was not possible, she decided numbly. One cannot live days and weeks of one's life under an assumption based on logic and fact, and then be told that the opposite is true. The clock cannot be turned back. Real events cannot be undone.

They rejected it, she reminded herself, loath to be carried aloft now by a bubble destined to burst. *It never had a chance.*

Unless Jack had lied.

Unless the *Journal* had been mistaken in its announcement of Avery Follett's nomination as architect.

Unless Reid had told the truth.

In a mist of bewilderment she was signing the cheque for her winnings. Robbie was helping her examine her score card before signing it, and repeating the improbable score over and over again, sixty-two, sixty-two, sixty-two. Inside the clubhouse the reporters' familiar faces loomed before her. She saw Ron Lieber, impassive and cold, regarding her with the ghost of a shrug.

'Miss Lake,' he asked, 'to what do you attribute this surprising turnaround . . .?'

'Ron,' said a laughing colleague whose fingers encircled his arm in a hard grip, 'give up!'

Lieber stepped back to take notes as the others called out questions.

But Joanna was too exhausted to answer.

'Don't worry, Jo,' came a friendly voice, 'we'll cover for you. Shall we say that you're tired but happy?'

It was Charlie Sullivan, his mild features lit by an avuncular smile. Joanna nodded, then touched his hand.

'The Black Woods,' she whispered. 'What happened? I didn't know . . .'

'They released it to the press this morning,' he told her. 'They accepted your design in a meeting yesterday. I don't know why nobody told you, Jo. Maybe they didn't want to bother you with it during your final round.' He raised an eyebrow. 'Would it have made a difference if you'd known before you went out on the course today?'

Stunned, she looked into his eyes. She would never know the answer to his question, and she was glad she would never know.

Moments later she was in the locker room, her knee stripped of its tape and receiving a desperately needed ice massage. Her fellow pros added their congratulations with quiet little hugs and pats, reminding her softly that she must get some rest. Aware now that she was in a state of physical and mental prostration, she dared not look at herself in the mirror.

In a few minutes she would call Tina. Then she would arrange somehow to get herself back to the hotel for a rest. Much later, after a decent interval of silence and oblivion, she would try to sort out what had happened to her today.

'Joanna?' A voice tore her from her reverie. 'I'm sorry to disturb you . . .'

She looked up to see the unfamiliar face of an attractive, middle-aged woman. Its features struck a distant chord. She thought she had seen it in a photograph somewhere.

'I'm Bettina Clarke,' the stranger smiled. 'We've met, but you probably don't remember me. It was at an L.P.G.A. meeting last year.'

'Oh,' stammered Joanna, cursing her forgetfulness. 'Of course. How are you?' Bettina Clarke was an L.P.G.A. official known for her work in tournament promotion.

'I know you must be all in,' she said, 'but I just wanted to tell you how delighted we all are over the Black Woods. It's a great step for women. And I want to add my personal word,' she added, brushing a lock of greying sunbleached hair from her brow. 'I saw your design, and it's absolutely the greatest.'

In confusion Joanna smiled. 'You saw it yourself?' she asked. 'How did . . .?'

'A man named Reid Armstrong showed it to me. He was lobbying everybody he could find in the organisation to have a look at it—on the quiet, so to speak. We all saw it, I think, over a period of days. It's been our best-kept secret ever since.'

At a loss for words, Joanna could only shake her head in perplexity.

'I'm really not clear on this,' she said at last. 'Did he say why . . .?'

'Oh, yes, he told us in detail. He said he knew there was going to be political trouble with the Black Woods committee if a woman was proposed as architect. He'd been sceptical himself, he said, until he actually saw what you'd conceived for the course. That convinced him, and he saw his job as simply making sure the inevitable happened sooner rather than later.'

Joanna smiled. 'He's such a confident man,' she said. 'It's not easy to say no to him. He wanted us to make a sort of formal, although confidential statement to the effect that when and if a course based on your design became a reality, the L.P.G.A. would endorse and work for a major tournament to be held on that site.'

Her brown eyes sparkled. 'His reasoning was obvious. If the Black Woods committee knew that your design would attract a major L.P.G.A. tournament, they would see important revenues coming in year after year, and a corresponding membership in their club. Well, we could hardly refuse after we studied the design. It's such a fantastic document, such a brilliant concept. We met last week and drafted the letter. I guess it did the trick—although I must say Reid Armstrong might have done without it if he had had to. I have a funny feeling he's been in contact with a lot of big-money sponsors already, and applying quiet pressure all over the place.'

Joanna was too tired to hide the truth. 'I thought my design had been rejected,' she said. 'I was sure of it.'

'You mean the Avery Follett business,' the other woman nodded. 'That was a political manoeuvre, I understand. It was engineered by a faction on the committee that was afraid no one would join the country club if the course was designed by a woman. They rushed through a vote when the other members had their backs turned, so to speak. Reid found out about it, of course, and he stayed in close touch with all the individuals involved and kept up the pressure. He even talked to Avery, who was perfectly aware that the offer they had made him was not firm.'

'I don't know what to say,' stammered Joanna. 'I'm in a state of shock.'

'I'm awfully sorry,' said Bettina, touching Joanna's hand. 'I thought you knew more about it all. I just assumed Reid would be keeping you informed.'

He tried to tell me, Joanna thought, her heart sinking.

'Well, he must have had his reasons,' concluded Bettina. 'Perhaps he didn't want to upset you with the sordid details of it all until he had good news to report. I got the distinct impression he wasn't particularly enamoured of the committee members or their friends. I think he relished the challenge of making them do what they didn't want to do.'

She had stood up to leave, but hesitated, her smile a trifle embarrassed.

'I suppose I should keep my big mouth shut,' she said, 'but my woman's instincts told me that Reid Armstrong has it pretty bad for you, Joanna.' She laughed. 'I'm sure he isn't alone in that, with your looks. But I think you have quite an admirer there. I know how hard he fought for you. The last thing he would want would be for you to be hurt. Anyway, all's well that ends well.'

A moment later she had gone, leaving Joanna alone with the hurtling avalanche of new thoughts which had overtaken her.

An hour ago she had believed she was alone in the world, and must depend entirely on her own initiative. That belief had fuelled each of the carefully calculated strokes that had won her the Tournament of Champions. Solitude, her inescapable fate, had at last seemed to come to her rescue on the golf course.

Now she had lost that most basic of assumptions. The rehabilitated body that had executed those winning shots, she realised, owed its strength and suppleness to Reid Armstrong. And the competitive spirit that had driven her onward, past the brilliant field at Maple Hills and finally past the great Peggy Byrne herself, came in large measure from Reid's impact on her.

Even the cold anger that had guided her strokes in pitiless concentration, forcing fear and pain into distant corners of her consciousness—even that owed its intensity to Reid.

Three months of her life wheeled before her mind's eye like the colours of a kaleidoscope. And there was no denying the pattern their days and nights formed now— the pattern Reid had predicted. She was a winner in competition, and her design for the Black Woods would become a reality.

'He told the truth,' she repeated to herself in amazement as the knee that had known his touch so many times bathed now in its ice.

When have I given you reason to doubt my word? His warning voice came back to her, perplexed and angry. And only now she could hear the hurt in its deep tones.

I don't know who's been putting ideas into your head . . .

Now the incredible truth was coiled mercilessly around her. Reid had asked her to believe in him for a few days and weeks, after having dedicated months of his life to her and to Tina. And she had turned away from him, investing her credence in the one man on earth most obviously motivated to hurt her: Jack Templeton.

Jack had come armed with tempting grains of truth to support his lies. There was something almost pathetic, in retrospect, about the little exhibits he had flourished in his triumph. Yes, she mused: they were damaging enough. But she should have seen through them when she realised it was not by accident that he had come back to interrupt her life.

Instead she had allowed his spiteful, petty perform-ance to compel her belief, to change the course of her existence—while the little girl who had never met Jack, the child who loved Reid Armstrong, played unwittingly only a room away.

For an instant Joanna almost forgave herself for turning that darkest of corners, as the letter signed by Carl Jaeger flashed across her memory. It had been easy to assume that the ultimate betrayal was possible, the final nightmare, once she had seen that letter.

And Jack must have assumed that in advance. Jack, who knew where she was most vulnerable. Jack, who had known Carl since his days as a player on the Georgia golf team—and who had perhaps solicited the letter himself as a member of the Black Woods committee.

Now the awful significance of Jack's membership in that hidebound group, thanks to the tentacles of his father's money, came home to Joanna. Undoubtedly it had caused him to cross paths with Reid at one time or another, and to know that Reid had offered the design commission to Joanna Lake.

But there was more to it than that. Joanna imagined the unsuspecting affability with which Reid must have lobbied the fearful committee members to accept her innovative design. He must have twisted their arms, cajoled and pressured them in his blithe way, without ever realising that among them was a man who was drawing his private inferences from everything that was said.

Unsuspecting, Reid must have worked for Joanna with all his skill. Was it possible that a trace of the tenderness she had seen so often in his tawny eyes might have been visible when he spoke of her before the committee? If Bettina Clarke had noticed that impalpable shade of emotion in him, why not the committee members?

I saw the picture of you with Reid on the golf course.

Joanna recalled the opening gambit in Jack's cruel assault on her. He had seen the photo snapped by the Beaufort journalist the day of her very first round of golf with Reid. Sold to a wire service, the picture had appeared in newspapers all over the country, showing Joanna shaking Reid's hand after defeating him with her final putt.

From her soft smile in that photograph Jack must have drawn the conclusion he had been tempted to draw from his own suspicions of Reid. And indeed, the picture had been taken only hours before Joanna had given herself to Reid, her senses on fire with the joyful knowledge that he wanted her and accepted her.

With halting breaths she sat now on the locker room table, seeing herself trapped in the frame of the photo which was visible to all the world, visible to those who might want to harm her, to harm Reid . . .

Confused, she thought how difficult it was to escape the clutches of the past. In breaking with his own family Reid had rejected the very society that had produced Jack. A society whose genteel surface was built on greed and venality, a society of cold, empty people who believed in nothing.

But Reid had believed in Joanna. And in committing himself to her so honestly, he had allowed the very forces he had spent a lifetime outwitting to take their revenge—in the form of Jack Templeton.

She shuddered to think that it was her own forgotten past which had come back to coil around her and, in that sinister crossroads, to fool her into turning against the only man who was on her side. Reid's mistake was to have placed his trust in her without arming himself against the dangers surrounding her. Dangers come from her past, which she herself could not see.

How strange to consider Reid's own vulnerability, she mused. Reid, who trusted no one, who could be manipulated by no one . . .

I don't know who's been putting ideas in your head.

Thunderstruck, Joanna gasped aloud.

'He knew!' she told herself in shock. 'He knew everything!'

Reid was a thorough man. He would research the background of anyone he came in contact with, including the committe members. Including Joanna herself!

He must have been aware that Jack Templeton was her ex-husband. And when the letter from Carl Jaeger was used as a pretext for rejecting her design, Reid must have seen it, known about it, and understood its real importance.

But he did not tell her, for obvious reasons.

It wasn't important. I didn't want to worry you about it when you had other things on your mind.

It all fitted. Reid considered himself Joanna's friend and protector. When he found out that the two men who had been closest to her were united against her, he could hardly be inclined to upset her with such terrible news.

Particularly when it was not news that in any way daunted him where her course design was concerned. Convinced as always of his own abilities, he must have simply resolved to see the design accepted, as he had promised—and to shield her from the dirty knowledge he possessed about Jack and Carl.

But then she had banished him cruelly, furiously, her pitiless words striking far deeper than her disappointment over the design could have justified.

Why beat a dead horse with your lies?

Why not get Tina out here? She doesn't know you as I do.

She dared not linger over that awful scene. But she knew now that under the worst of insults Reid's sense of honour had decreed that he not stoop to defend himself by denouncing others. Deeply hurt by Joanna, he would not hurt her back.

And after that night he had continued his efforts on

behalf of her design, and had achieved the success he counted on from the beginning.

Wherever he was now, he must be thinking that he had at least proved he had been true to his word. Powerless to oppose Joanna's stupid incredulity through argument, he had done so by bringing about a reality she could not deny.

'What must he think of me now?' she reflected miserably in the solitude of the locker room. 'After all he did . . .'

Conflicting ideas tormented her as she considered her situation. Her own sense of fairness required that she apologise to Reid. Yet no apology could undo the damage done by her horrid, cruel words the night he had appeared at her house. And no kindly destiny could unravel the dark threads of chaos that had coaxed those words from her lips, sealing her doom as they bound her once more to her unhappy solitude.

But the unspoken thought taking shape in her mind outstripped despair itself as it lifted her from the table and propelled her with irresistible urgency towards the telephone. Indifferent to the pain in her leg, she fumbled in her purse for her credit card. Moving like a sleepwalker, she found coins and a telephone number.

If Bettina Clarke had seen that impalpable light of tenderness in Reid's complex eyes when he spoke of Joanna, it could not be entirely non-existent. If Jack had used his knowledge of it as a weapon in his own intrigues, it must have been real.

And Joanna herself had spent bittersweet weeks of ecstasy and heartbreak believing in that light even as she forced herself to renounce it.

How could it have been a mere illusion? People saw it. It had effects in the real world.

'Reservations,' came the voice on the phone. 'Can I help you?'

'I hope so,' said Joanna. 'I have a reservation for tomorrow morning's flight to Sarasota. Could I get on a flight to Savannah tonight? And I'd like to rent a car, please.'

She turned to look at the locker room. It seemed as foreign a landscape as her own life. The centre of gravity of her whole existence was outside her now, exiled in a distant house on a hill overlooking the ocean.

She trembled with anticipation, her fingers crossed desperately, as she waited for the voice to come back on the line.

For she was no stranger to impermanence.

A light may be real, she knew, and still go out.

Hours later, oblivious to the unutterable fatigue her decision had brought upon her, Joanna closed the door of her rented car and stood in the darkness outside Reid's house.

She could hear the hushed boom of the surf on the beach beyond the bridle paths. Under her feet was the driveway on which she had stood when she said goodbye to Reid while Tina watched. She could still feel the impotent message of love and renunciation that had quickened in her fingertips as they touched his hard back that day.

The Southern night was balmy and lit by stars. Before Joanna stood the jeep which had driven her to the Black Woods so often, and been her accomplice the day of her furtive excursion to the driving range. Beside it was the big sedan in which she had slept on the long journey from Fayetteville.

On the distant beach Tina had played with Katie and swum under Reid's watchful eye while her mother jogged or rode her bicycle along the trails that crisscrossed these hills. In the quiet air over the lawn

Joanna could still hear the little shout of glee that came from Tina's lips as Reid had swooped her up, a giddy packet of vibrant energy, for a ride on his shoulders.

Behind the shadowed sights and sounds that greeted her under this starry sky were all the invisible threads that had joined together over the stately passage of the days to create her beautiful, painful summer. They were made of laughter and worry and well-kept secrets, those threads—and most of all they were made of hope.

And even now she could feel the million unseen dreams and yearnings that had come from the remotest times of her life to knit themselves into that shimmering fabric of summer, only to be torn away by her cautious hand when she left this place.

She forced herself to look back at the cars. They were both here. That meant he was home. Taking a deep breath, she approached the door.

It began to open before she reached it. Too late she realised the sound of her car must have been heard inside at this silent hour. In a flash she thought of the private life she was about to disturb.

Reid stood before her, framed by the light of the vestibule behind him. He was dressed in jeans and a sports shirt which hugged the muscled contours of his body.

Try as she might, she could not move a step closer to him. For an instant she saw indescribable emotion, quick and intense, in his dark eyes. Then he leaned casually against the door frame, his arms folded, his old humour come to stand between him and his visitor.

'What brings you here?' he asked.

The words that stirred on her lips were not those she had planned to say. Like a mystery they came, foreign things that did not belong to her. Yet she knew she must not hold them back.

'I need someone,' she began unsteadily, meeting his

gaze with the last of her courage. 'Someone to watch out for me.'

His smile touched her softly as he looked down upon her. But he was shaking his head.

'No, you don't,' he said. 'You don't need anyone, Joanna. You're a winner.'

Her heart sank within her breast. She could feel his strength arming him to free her.

'Unless,' he said, 'you mean someone to rub your sore knee and see that you get your rest. Someone to make sure you don't jump to conclusions about who your real friends are . . .'

He had stepped forward, placing gentle hands on her shoulders. 'Someone to be a father to that little girl of yours,' he said. 'Someone to marry you, and love you for ever, so that you'll never, never be alone again . . .'

She was in his arms, home at last, it seemed, for the first time in her memory. His lips were against her hair, and she heard them murmur truths that warmed her like the tenderest of caresses.

'I was in love with you long before there was a Black Woods golf course to design,' he said. 'I fell in love with you from watching you play golf on television. When I saw the chance to meet you, I jumped at it. How was I to know that my meddling in your life was practically going to get you killed, and ruin your career and leave you scarred and injured?' He shook his head. 'I was happy to see you win today, because it at least meant you were whole again, even if I'd lost you.'

'No,' Joanna whispered. 'Not whole. Not without you.'

He glanced past her at the driveway. 'I hated to let you go this summer,' he said. 'I wanted us to be together, but I didn't dare ask where we stood.'

She nodded against his chest, too overcome to tell him how deeply she had shared his anguish.

'So you didn't mean . . .?' he asked, his words calling up the most terrible of all the obstacles that had separated them.

'I love you,' she said, clasping him to her with all her strength. 'I've always loved you.' She brushed his lips with her own, her hands in his hair and around his neck, her heart bursting with a reality she could not contain. 'Forgive me.'

'For standing on your own two feet when you knew you had to?' Reid shook his head. 'That's nothing to forgive, Joanna. And as for being slow to realise that the time for going it alone was past—I'm no stranger to that mistake myself. But it's all behind us now, isn't it?'

She held him closer still, as though to draw courage from him for the last step she knew she must take in order to be his.

'Yes,' she said, 'it's behind us.'

'For ever?'

The future had come alive within her breast, triumphant and infinite as it banished the world to which she had clung with all her might for so long. And the pain of being swept up that way might have torn her apart, had she not felt herself safe and secure in the arms that held her now, their power coursing through her boundlessly.

She saw herself mirrored in his smiling eyes, no longer the solitary woman who had fought so desperately to remain on her own, but eclipsed now by someone new, someone capable of opening herself to him joyfully and completely. And all at once the last step seemed gentle and easy, as though she had known the way from the beginning, but lost it somehow, until this quiet night and these strong arms could show it to her once more.

'For ever,' she said.

4 FREE
Harlequin Romances

TAKE THESE 4 Harlequin Romances FREE

Delight in **Mary Wibberley**'s warm romance, MAN OF POWER, the story of a girl whose life changes from drudgery to glamour overnight....Let THE WINDS OF WINTER by **Sandra Field** take you on a journey of love to Canada's beautiful Maritimes....Thrill to a cruise in the tropics—and a devastating love affair in the aftermath of a shipwreck—in **Rebecca Stratton**'s THE LEO MAN.... Travel to the wilds of Kenya in a quest for love with the determined heroine in **Karen van der Zee**'s LOVE BEYOND REASON.

Harlequin Romances . . . 6 exciting novels published each month! Each month you will get to know interesting, appealing, true-to-life people . . . . You'll be swept to distant lands you've dreamed of visiting . . . . Intrigue, adventure, romance, and the destiny of many lives will thrill you through each Harlequin Romance novel.

Get all the latest books before they're sold out!

As a Harlequin subscriber you actually receive your personal copies of the latest Romances immediately after they come off the press, so you're sure of getting all 6 each month.

Cancel your subscription whenever you wish!

You don't have to buy any minimum number of books. Whenever you decide to stop your subscription just let us know and we'll cancel all further shipments.